THE POET'S HOMECOMING

Footprints

One night a man had a dream. He dreamed he was walking along the beach with the Lord. Across the sky flashed scenes from his life. For each scene, he noticed two sets of footprints in the sand: one belonging to him, and the other to the Lord.

When the last scene of his life flashed before him, he looked back at the footprints in the sand. He noticed that many times along the path of his life there was only one set of footprints. He also noticed that it happened at the very lowest and saddest times in his life.

This really bothered him and he questioned the Lord about it.

"Lord, you said that once I decided to follow you, you'd walk with me all the way. But I have noticed that during the most troublesome times in my life, there is only one set of footprints. I don't understand why when I needed you the most you would leave me."

The Lord replied, "My son, My precious child, I love you and would never leave you. During your times of trial and suffering, when you see only one set of footprints, it was then that I carried you."

Author unknown

THIS BOOK BELONGS TO

Stephanie Kennedy

B161 ©APCo

THE POET'S HOMECOMING

GEORGE MACDONALD

MICHAEL R. PHILLIPS, EDITOR

BETHANY HOUSE PUBLISHERS
MINNEAPOLIS, MINNESOTA 55438

Originally published as *Home Again* in 1887
by Kegan, Paul, Trench, Trubner & Co., London.

Copyright © 1990 .
Michael R. Phillips
All Rights Reserved

Published by Bethany House Publishers
A Ministry of Bethany Fellowship, Inc.
6820 Auto Club Road, Minneapolis, Minnesota 55438

Printed in the United States of America

Library of Congress Cataloging-in-Publication Data

MacDonald, George, 1824–1905.
   [Home again]
   The poet's homecoming / George MacDonald : edited by
Michael R. Phillips.
      p.   cm.
   "Originally published as Home again in 1887 by Kegan, Paul, Trench,
Trubner & Co., London."
   I. Phillips, Michael R.   II. Title.
[PR4967.H6   1990]
823'.8—dc20   90–421
ISBN 1–55661–135–8   CIP

I dedicate my own small contribution to this new edition of
Home Again to a writer well acquainted—
like the poet of this tale—
with the disappointments and triumphs of an author's life,
who knows also the nature of our
true calling beyond earthly recognition—

Nick Harrison,

friend, co-worker, and sharer in the vision
of what life in God is meant to be.

Contents

8

Introduction

During the first years of our reading of George MacDonald's books, my wife and I fairly devoured everything we could lay our hands on. After a year or two, the realization suddenly broke upon me that if we continued at such a pace the supply would exhaust itself within a very short time. One of the great regrets of my life is that I will never again be able to read *Narnia* for the first time. Rereading a favorite book is a good thing, but certain literary first loves are never the same the second time around!

Therefore, I made a determined effort to slow the pace, saying to myself that I wanted to reserve some of MacDonald's books for later, so that, even in my old age, there would still be a few treasures I could bring out of my storehouse and look forward to with that relish of discovery only a new book can bring.

This adventure of editing and reissuing MacDonald's books, however, proved a turn in my life I hadn't foreseen, and both publication necessity and the desire to share his books with others have served to accelerate the strategy I had established for myself. Thus, before launching into this present book, I found myself, with mingled anticipation and regret, facing the *last* of MacDonald's adult novels I had not yet read. It represented almost the end of a very personal odyssey of discovery that was tinged with sadness. I had not "planned" to allow myself to dive into this book till I was sixty at least! Consequently, as I went through this volume, I found myself relishing the words and sentences and ideas—I can't say more, but certainly with a reinvigorated sense of awe—as I beheld anew the wisdom to which God opened this man, his servant. And when I reached the last page, a quiet sense of completion came over me. In nineteen years I have read thirty-five works of George MacDonald's fiction, finishing them perhaps sooner than I had hoped, yet with an abiding thankfulness to God for the opportunities that have arisen to share these treasures with you.

And now I have the opportunity to spend the *next* twenty years not only rereading but also learning more deeply to *live* the spiritual principles of practical faith about which George MacDonald wrote. For those truths are *ever* new—whether I be in my 20's, my 40's, or my 60's. Age and familiarity bring no loss to their immediacy!

So while the plots may never be new again, perhaps that is fitting. Because the plots are not that for which MacDonald wrote, but rather for the living truths which undergird them. I don't know about you, but I find it easy to be carried away mentally with MacDonald's insights and little "gems" of truth. I run around excitedly, fluttering here and there like poor Mrs. Evermore on the lookout for fanciful notions, thinking in vain I can bottle up MacDonald's perceptions, to reread and underline and put down in my notebook as particularly quotable. Thus I must make it my constant prayer that I will resist this all-too-human tendency, and will become more and more keenly conscious as I read that the truths to which he points are things I must *do*.

Of course that process is a continually unfolding one, as I'm sure you find it in your life too. After all these years reading and working with the books and ideas of George MacDonald, I feel I am just beginning to get the picture of God he was attempting to convey. Working recently on the two books *Discovering the Character of God* and *Knowing the Heart of God* has opened huge new vistas in my spiritual being. Having read over thirty of MacDonald's novels, and being, as I thought, somewhat familiar with his fiction, it was not until I began these two works (taken predominately from his written sermons) that a number of inner lights began to explode within me.

"I can't believe it!" I found myself saying any number of times. "So *that's* what you've been trying to get through to me!

But . . . but . . . this is astonishing! Do you mean to say God is really *that* loving . . . *that* wonderful . . . *that* involved in the tiniest detail of my life *and* in the myriad forces of nature all about me! It's too huge . . . it's more than my brain can comprehend!''

Over and over I found myself breaking one moment into laughter, another into tears, another into prayers of conviction over my own shallowness—brought painfully face to face with how far I yet have to go before I really "know" God as He desires me to know him. Once I simply turned off my typewriter, got up, and went immediately home, sat my family down, and confessed my need of their prayers. We then went before the Lord together, my wife and three sons laying their hands on me and praying for this man who was supposed to be their spiritual guide, but who was at that moment feeling a million miles off from the inner Christlikeness which was his heart's desire. In short, it's impossible to convey the extent to which those two books (and indeed *all* the MacDonald books I have read and worked on) have impacted my whole outlook on God's being and his remaking work in my life!

This present volume, *The Poet's Homecoming,* is an intrinsic part of that learning process. As I said, reaching the end of a long list of "stories," I am realizing anew my need, not for new plots, but for deeper levels of obedience in my attitudes and behavior and relationships. After many years of scratching away through surface concerns and appearances, it is my prayer that perhaps now God can penetrate to serious levels of self-denial in my spirit. Such remains my prayer.

Like *The Landlady's Master, The Poet's Homecoming* is an extremely rare title to locate in its original (*Home Again*), and one of MacDonald's later (1887) and more obscure titles. It is not a long book, nor a particularly detailed one. Yet perhaps because of that, the radiance of the message shines through with unclouded clarity—the message that, as MacDonald himself says, obedience is the opener of eyes. And some of the specifics of that message as it emerges through the characters of this story are particularly meaningful to me in light of my relationships with my own sons and my own father. This book was written at a time when five of MacDonald's six sons were in their early to mid-twenties, and he himself was no doubt at the time pondering many of the parental struggles involved in watching one's children grow and stumble and mature into adulthood. Many times as I read I found myself filled anew with gratitude to both my fathers, for indeed my heavenly Father has given me an earthly father not unlike Richard Colman of *Home Again.*

No, this story is not a complicated one. Yet sometimes the profoundest truths come wrapped in the humblest garb. When first told by the Master in Luke 10, this tale was not noteworthy for its complexity but for its disarming simplicity. And it thus remains one of the Lord's most striking teachings. MacDonald, too, when attempting to convey the magnificence of God's Fatherhood, does so with acuity of vision and simplicity of word. For to MacDonald that truth was the first truth, the foundational truth, the most vital truth for man and woman to apprehend. It is a truth to be seen at root in every story, every sermon, every poem he wrote, and here he makes it the core of his message.

Michael Phillips

1 / Father and Aunt

In the dusk of the old-fashioned best room of a farmhouse, in the faint glow of the buried sun through the sods of his July grave, two dimly visible elderly persons sat breathing the odor which roses unseen sent through the twilight and open window. One of the two was scarcely conscious of the sweet fragrance, for she did not believe in roses. She believed mainly in mahogany, linen, and hams. To the other it brought too much sadness to be welcomed, for like the sunlight it seemed to come from the grave of his vanished youth.

Richard Colman was not by nature a sad man. He was only one who had found the past more delightful than the present, and had not left his first loves. The twilight of his years had crept upon him and was steadily deepening, and he felt his youth slowly withering under their fallen leaves. With more education, and perhaps more receptivity than most farmers, he had married a woman he fervently loved. Her rare truthful nature, to which throughout her life she had striven to keep true, had developed the delicate flower of moral and social refinement, and her influence upon him had been of the eternal sort.

While many of their neighbors were vying with each other in the vain effort to dress, and dwell, and live up to their notion of gentility, each in the eyes of the other, Richard Colman and his wife had never troubled themselves about fashion or opinion or what is commonly called "getting ahead," but had each sought to please the taste of the other and cultivate their own. Perhaps now as he sat thus, silent in the twilight, he was holding closer communion than he knew, or any of us can know, with one who

13

seemed to have vanished from all this side of things—except the heart of her husband, which clung to what people would call her memory; I prefer to call it her.

The rose-scented hush was torn by the strident, shrill, self-confident, and self-satisfied voice of his dead wife's half sister, who seemed to think it her duty to look after Mrs. Colman's interests after her passing.

"Richard," she said, "that son of yours will come to no good! You may take my word for it! He is hardly fit to be called his mother's son."

Mr. Colman made no answer. The dusky, sweet-smelling waves of the silence closed over the wound that had been made in it by the high-pitched female voice.

"I am well aware that my opinion is of no value in your eyes, Richard," she went on after but a moment, "but that does not absolve me from the duty of stating it, in respect of my sister, God rest her soul: if you allow him to go on as he is now doing, Walter will never eat bread of his own earning, nor ever amount to anything in this world!"

There are many who do earn their own bread, yet still don't come to much in the end, thought the father to himself.

"What do you mean to make of him?" persisted Miss Hancock, the *a* in whose name Walter said ought to have been an *e*.

"Whatever he is able to make himself. He must have the main hand in it, whatever it be," answered Mr. Colman.

"It is long past the time he should have set about something! He is old enough to be working and supporting himself! You let him go on dawdling and dawdling, without so much as a hint of his making up his mind whether or not he ought to do anything. Take my word for it, Richard, you'll have him on your hands till the day of your death."

The father did not reply that he could wish for nothing better, and that the threat was more than he could hope for. He did not want to provoke his sister-in-law. Besides, he knew there was a shadow of reason in what she said, though even perfect reason could not have sweetened the mode in which she said it. Nothing could make up for the total absence of sympathy in her utterance of any modicum of truth she was capable of uttering.

Ann Hancock was a very dusty woman, and never more dusty than when she fought against dust as in a warfare worthy of all a woman's energies—one who, because she had not a spark of Mary in her, imagined herself a Martha. She was true as steel to the interests of those in whose life hers was involved, but only their dusty interests, not those which make man worth God's trouble. She was a vessel of clay in an outhouse of the temple, and took on her the airs—not of gold, for gold has no airs—but the airs of clay imagining itself gold, and all the golden vessels nothing but clay.

"I put it to you, Richard Colman," she went on, "did any good ever come of reading poetry, and falling asleep under haystacks! He actually writes poetry, that son of yours!—and we all know what that leads to!"

"Do we?" ventured her brother-in-law. "King David wrote poetry."

"Don't twist my words, Richard. You know what I mean as well as I do myself. And you know as well what comes of writing poetry! That friend of Walter's who borrowed ten pounds from you—did he ever repay you?"

"He did."

"You didn't tell *me*!"

"I did not want to disappoint your judgment of him," replied Mr. Colman with a sarcasm she did not note.

"I wish I had known," she returned. "It was worth telling."

"I did not think so. Everybody does not stick to a bank note like a snail to the wall. And I did not think the matter would interest you, after all, for I returned him the money."

"Returned him the money!"

"Yes."

"Made him a gift of ten pounds!"

"Yes—why not?"

"I should ask you *why*?"

"I had more reasons than one."

"And no call to explain them! That is just like you to throw away your hard earnings upon a fellow who will no doubt never earn anything for himself. As if one lazy poet son wasn't enough to take all you'd got—now you're giving your money to his ne'er-do-well friends besides!"

"How could the young man send me back the money if he was as you say? No, he proved himself what I believed him—ready and willing to work. The money went for a fellow's bread and cheese, and what better money's worth would you have? I do not grudge my investment in my son's friend."

"You may someday want the bread and cheese for yourself!"

"One stomach is as good as another."

"It will never be any use trying to talk to some people!" concluded Ann, in the same tone in which she had begun, for she seldom lost her temper—though no one would have much minded her losing it, seeing it was so little worth keeping. Rarely angry, she was always disagreeable. The good that was in her had no flower, but bore its fruits in the shape of good food, clean linen, mended socks, and such, without any blossom of sweet graciousness to make life pleasant.

Walter's aunt Ann would have been quite justified in looking on poetry with contempt had it been what she imagined it. Like many others, she held definite opinions on many things of which her idea in no way corresponded with the things themselves.

2 / Another Conversation in the Arbor_____

While the elders thus conversed in the dusky drawing room, overpowered by the smell of old roses, another couple sat in a little homely foliage-covered shelter in the garden. It was in fact the subject of the other conversation, Richard's son Walter, who occupied the wooden bench-seat with his rather distant cousin, Molly Wentworth. The two for fifteen years had been as brother and sister.

The fathers of the two young people had been great friends. When Molly's died in India, and a year or two later her mother followed him, Richard Colman took the little orphan Molly, who was at the time with a nurse in England and without other relations, home to his house, much to the joy of his wife, who had often longed for a daughter to grow up with their one son, and thus perfect the family idea. The more motherly a woman is, the nearer will the child of another satisfy the necessities of her motherhood. In time, Mrs. Colman could hardly have said which child she loved best.

A weight of peace rested over the still summer garden. It was a night to the very mind of the twilight-loving bat, flitting about, coming and going, like a thought we cannot help.

Most of Walter's thoughts came and went in such seemingly random fashion. He had not yet learned to think. He was hardly more than a passive medium in which thought came and went. Yet when a thought seemed worth anything, he always gave himself credit for it—as if a man were author of his own thoughts as much as of his own existence! A man can but live so with the life given him that this or that kind of thoughts shall call on him, and to this or that kind he shall or shall not be at home. Walter was only at that early stage of development where a man is in love with what he calls his own thoughts; he was not yet conscious of a higher power to which he owed not only what he now called himself, but his very breath as well.

Even in the dark of the summer house one might have seen that he was pale, and might have suspected him handsome. In the daylight his gray eyes might almost seem the source of his paleness. His features were well marked, though delicate, and possessed a notable look of distinction. He was above average height and slenderly built, had a wide forehead, and wore a small, light moustache on an otherwise smooth face. His mouth was the least interesting feature of his countenance. It had great mobility, but when at rest contained little shape and no attraction. For this, however, his smile made considerable amends.

The girl was dark, almost swarthy, with the clear pure complexion and fine-grained skin that more commonly accompany the hue. If at first she gave the impression of delicacy, it soon changed into one of compressed life, of latent power. Through the night, where she now sat, her eyes were too dark to appear. They sank into the gathering gloom, and were as the unseen soul of the dark, while her mouth, rather large and exquisitely shaped with the curve of a strong bow, seemed as often as she smiled to make a pale window in the blackness. Her hair came rather low down the steep of her forehead, and, with the strength of her chin, made her face look rounder than seemed fitting.

They sat for a time as silent as the night that enfolded them. They were not lovers, though they loved one another, perhaps more than either knew. They were watching to see the head of the valley on one of whose high sloping sides they sat.

The moon kept her tryst, and revealed a loveliness beyond what the day had to show. As she rose, she looked upon a wide valley that gleamed with the reflected windings of a river. She brightened the shimmering flow of water, and dimmed in the houses and cottages the lights with which the opposite hill sparkled like a celestial map. She did her work lovely in the heavens, her poor mirror-work—all she was fit for, affording occasion, atmosphere, and medium to young imaginations unable yet to spread their wings in the sunlight and believe what lies hidden in the light of the workaday world.

Nor was what she revealed the less true for what lay unshown in the night. The vulgar cry for the real would bury every eternal fact in deepest grave. It is the cry, shouted unknowingly anew in every generation, "Not this man, but Barabbas!" Rather than the apparent beauty of this evening, the day would reveal instead a river stained with loathsome refuse, and rich gardens on hillsides mantled in sooty smoke and smelly vapors, sent up from a valley where men, like gnomes, toiled and caused others to toil too eagerly.

What would one think of a housekeeper so intent upon saving that she would waste no time on beauty or cleanliness? How pleasant would her house be to live in? Yet how many who would storm and fuss if they came home to an untidy house would feel no shadow of uneasiness that they have all day long been defiling their own houses, the house of the Father, and at night never lift a hand to cleanse it! Such men regard him as a fool, whose joy a foul river can poison; yet as soon as they have by pollution gathered and saved their god, they make haste to depart from the spot they have ruined. Oh for an invasion of indignant ghosts to drive from the old places the generation that dishonors the ancient Earth! The sun shows all their disfiguring, but the friendly night comes at length to hide her disgrace; and that well hidden, slowly ascends the brooding moon to unveil her beauty.

There was indeed a thriving town full of awful chimneys in the valley, and the clouds that rose from it ascended above the Colmans' farm to the great moor that stretched miles and miles beyond it. In the autumn sun its low forest of heather burned purple, while in the pale winter it lay white under snow and frost. But through all the year winds would blow across it the dull smell of the smoke from below. Had such a polluting fume risen to the earthly paradise, Dante would have imagined his purgatory sinking into hell. On all this inferno the night had now sunk like a foretaste of cleansing death. The fires lay smoldering like poor helpless devils, fain to sleep. The world was merged in a tidal wave from the ocean of hope, and seemed to heave a restful sigh under its cooling renovation.

"A penny for your thought, Walter," said the girl after a long silence, in which the night seemed at length to clasp her too close.

"I was thinking," he replied, "how wild and sweet the dark wind would be blowing up there among the ringing bells of heather."

"Oh, that is a beautiful notion! You shall have the penny, and I will have my money's worth."

Walter laughed.

"I will pay you with your own coin," Molly went on, her white teeth reflecting the moon with her smile. "I keep all the pennies I win from you. What do you do with those you win from me?"

"Oh, I don't know. I only take them because you insist on paying your bets, but—"

"Debts you mean, Walter. You know I never bet, even in fun. I would not take something for nothing."

"Then what are you making me do now?"

"Take a penny for the thought I bought from you for a penny. That's a fair trade, not gambling. Especially tonight. Your thought is easily the value of a penny—I felt the very wind on the moor for a moment."

"I'm afraid I won't get a penny a thought in London!"

"Then you really are going, Walter?"

"What else can I do? I must get on with my life sometime, and what is a man to do here?"

"There is plenty of work to be found in the fields or in town."

"Work perhaps. But no future. Certainly no future for a writer."

"And what is a man to do in London?"

"Meet people, find opportunities—make his way in the world."

"Please, Walter, I truly want to understand. But what is it you wish to make your way to?"

"Why, to—to such a position as—" Here he stopped, unsure.

"You mean to fame and honor and riches, Walter?" ventured Molly.

"No—not riches. It is not money I want. Did you ever hear of a poet and riches in the same breath?"

"Yes, I have—though they don't exactly seem to go comfortably together. But if not riches, where does the way you speak of lead, then, Walter? To fame?"

"If it did, what would you have to say against it? Is fame a bad thing in itself? Even Milton calls it 'That last infirmity of a noble mind.' "

"But as you say, he does call it an infirmity, and such a bad infirmity, apparently, that it is the hardest of all to get rid of!"

The fact was that Walter wanted to be—in fact thought he was—a poet. But he was far enough from certain of it, and deep inside feared indeed that it might not be so that he therefore was too desirous for the verdict of men in his favor. Fame was precious to him as determining, he thought, his position in the world of letters—his own personal kingdom of heaven. Though he was well-read, he had not used his reading practically enough to perceive that the praise of one generation may be the contempt of another, perhaps of the very next, so that the repute of his time could assure him of nothing. He had not yet come to realize the worthlessness of the opinion that either grants or withholds fame.

He looked through the dark at his cousin. She read his thought through the silence, and before he could formulate a reply, Molly spoke again.

"I know what you are thinking, Walter," she said. "You are wondering how I can talk of such things when women aren't supposed to be able to think. But what I have said is mere common sense, and I cannot see the sense of doing anything for a praise that can help nothing and settle nothing."

"Why then do all men desire it?"

"That they may get rid of it. Why do all men have vanity?

Where would the world be on the way to now if Jesus Christ had sought the praise of men?"

"But he does have it."

"Not much of it yet, I suspect. And most of what praise he does have amounts to nothing. He does not care for the praise that comes before obedience. I have heard your father say that very thing."

"I've never heard him."

"I have heard him say it often. Perhaps you have not heard him just because he *is* your father."

Walter did not reply. He did not find it comfortable to be offered counsel by his cousin. And a woman at that!

"What could Jesus possibly care for the praise of one whose object in life was the praise of men?" Molly asked, in a tone as if completing the previous thought. But again Walter said nothing.

Young Walter Colman had not lived so as to destroy the reverence of his childhood. He believed himself to have high ideals. He felt that a man ought to be upright. So strongly did he feel it that he imagined he was himself therefore upright, and thus incapable of a mean or dishonest thing. Because he thought uprightness a good thing, he considered that he must therefore be upright himself. And in all fairness to him, at this point in his life he had never done anything grossly unfair. As to his thought that he never could do such would remain for time to tell.

But to what Molly said, he had no answer. What he half thought in his silence was something like this: Jesus Christ was not the type of manhood, but just a man by himself, who came to do a certain work; came from God, he may have, but his was an isolated work, not the pattern for all men and women to follow. He considered it both absurd and irreverent to talk as if other men had to do as Jesus did, to think and feel like him. Jesus was so high above the world that he could not care for its fame, while to mere man its praises must be dear. To compare Jesus to his present case was ridiculous. Nor did Walter make any correct distinction between the approbation of understanding men, who know the thing they praise, and the empty voice of the unknowing and unwise masses.

In a word, Walter thought, without knowing he did, that Jesus Christ was not truly a man.

"I think, Molly," he said, "we had better avoid the danger of irreverence." For the sake of his poor reverence, which was in reality no reverence at all, he would frustrate the mission of the Son of God. By its mockery he would justify himself in refusing the judgment of Jesus.

"I know you think kindly of me, Molly," he went on, "and I would be sorry to have you misunderstand me. But surely a man should not require religion to make him honest. A man must be true because he is a man, whatever he believes. For my own honor, I shall at least do nothing disgraceful, however I may fall short of the angelic."

"I doubt whether a man is a man until he truly knows God," murmured Molly.

But if Walter heard the words, he neither heeded nor answered them. He was far from understanding the absurdity of doing right from love of self.

He was no hypocrite. If something seemed to him degrading he would turn from it. But there were things degrading that he did not see to be such, things on which some men to whom he did not yet look up to would have looked down on. Also there was that in his effort to sustain his self-respect which was far from pure: he despised those who failed, and to despise any human because he has fallen is to fall from the human oneself. He had done many little things he ought to be, and one day must be, but as yet felt no occasion to be, ashamed of. So long as they did not trouble him they seemed nowhere.

Many a youth starts in life in this manner, possessed with the idea, not exactly formulated, that he is a most precious specimen of pure and honorable humanity. Alas, how many years it takes on this earth before we begin but a little to know ourselves! Such a notion comes of self-ignorance and a low ideal taken for a high one. Such youths are usually well-behaved, well-thought-of, and never doubt themselves a prize for any woman. They color their notion of themselves with their ideal, and then mistake the one for the other. The mass of weaknesses and conceits that compose their being they compress into their ideal mold of man, and then regard the shape as their own. They never look inside to see what they are really made of!

No one, however, would have looked into the refined face of Walter Colman and imagined him cherishing sordid views of life. Asked what of all things he most admired, he might truly answer, "The imaginative intellect." He was a fledgling poet. He worshiped what he called thoughts, and would rave about a thought in the abstract, apostrophize an uncaught idea. When a concrete thinkable one fell to him, he was jubilant over the isolate thing. But his joy had nothing to do with its value or any practical result. Of the *doing* of any action as a necessary result of some thought or idea, Walter never considered the possibility. Thoughts and actions were to him as separate as night and day. That thoughts might *demand* action would have been an idea to him unthinkable. What could the one possibly have to do with the other?

For Walter, the thought *itself*—isolated, alone, hanging in space a beautiful thing to be looked at—was all in all. He would stand rapt in the delight of what he counted the beauty of some idea, and yet more in the delight that his was the mind that had generated such a meteor! To be able to think pretty things was to him a gigantic distinction that separated men and women. A thought that could never be soul to any action would be more valuable to him than the perception of some vitality of relation demanding the activity of the whole being. He would call thoughts the stars that glorify the firmament of humanity, but the stars of his firmament were merely atmospheric—pretty fancies, external likenesses that could never be *true* any more than the moon now looking down on them was the true source of the light shining from it. That the grandest thing in the world is to be an accepted writer is the foolish goal of a vast number of the weak-minded and half-made of both sexes. It feeds poetic fountains of plentiful yield, but insipid and enfeebling flow, the mere sweat of weakness under the stimulus of self-admiration.

Walter was the very opposite of the Molly he counted so

commonplace, one outside the region of poetry. For she had a passion for turning a *think* into a *thing*. She had a strong instinctive feeling that she was in the world to do something, and she saw that if nobody tried to keep things right, they would go terribly wrong. What then could she be there for but to help keep things right? And if she could do nothing with the big things, she must be the busier with the little things! Besides, who could tell how much the little might have to do with the big things. The whole machine depended on every tiny wheel. She could not order the clouds, but she could keep some weeds from growing, and when the rain came, they would not take away the good of it.

The world might be divided into those who let things go, and those who do not; into the forces and facts, and the slaves and fancies; into those who are always doing something on God's creative lines, and those who are always grumbling and striving against them.

"Another penny for your thought, Walter!" said Molly after a minute or two of silence.

"This time I do not think you would find it worth a penny. Why are you so inquisitive about my thoughts anyway?"

"I want to know what you meant when you said the other day that thoughts were better than things."

Walter hesitated. The question was an inclined plane leading to unknown depths of argument.

"See, Walter," said Molly, holding a flower out toward him in the deepened twilight, "here is a narcissus—a pheasant's eye. Tell me the thought that is better than this thing."

How troublesome girls were when they asked questions!

"Well," he said, not very logically, "that narcissus has nothing but air around it. But my thought of the narcissus has mind around it."

"Then a thought is better than a thing because it has thought around it?"

"Well, yes."

"Did the thing come there of itself, or did it come of God's thinking?"

"Of God's thinking, of course."

"And God is always the same?"

"Yes."

"Then God's thought is still about the narcissus—and the narcissus is better than your thought of it."

Walter was silent.

"I really would like to understand," said Molly. "If you have a thought more beautiful than the narcissus, Walter, I should like to see it! Only if I could see it, it would be a thing, wouldn't it? A *thing* must be a *think* before it can be a thing. A thing is a ripe think, and must be better than the mere idea of it—except it lose something in ripening—which may very well be with man's thoughts but hardly with God's. I will keep in front of the things, and look through them to the thoughts behind them. I do want to understand! If a thing were not a thought first, it would not be worth anything. And every thing has to be thought about, otherwise we don't see what it is. Yet the thought alone, before it has ripened into the thing it was made to become, doesn't seem to have value all by itself. But I still haven't got it quite right!"

Instead of replying, Walter rose, and they walked to the house side by side in silence.

"Could a thought be worth anything that God had never cared to think?" said Molly to herself as they went.

3 / Flutterbies

Mr. Colman and his adopted daughter were such fast and near friends that they could talk together about everything—including Walter, though he was but the adoptive brother of the one, and the real son of the other. Richard had inherited his wife's love for Molly and added it to his own. But their union had its root in the perfect truthfulness of the two. Real approximation, real human closeness and union must ever be in proportion to mutual transparency and truthfulness.

Thus, it was quite after the usual custom between the two for Molly to tell her father about the conversation she had with Walter.

"What first made you think of such a difference between thoughts and things, Molly?" asked Mr. Colman.

"I remember quite well," answered Molly. "You remember our visit to your old school friend, Mr. Dobson?"

"Of course—perfectly."

"And you remember Mrs. Evermore?"

"Yes."

"You thought her name a funny one. But you said it ought to have been 'Nevermore' because she seemed never to get any farther!"

Mr. Colman laughed. "Come, come, Molly!" he said. "That won't do! It was you, not I, who said it!"

"It was true anyway!" answered Molly, "and you agreed with me. So if I said it first, you said it last. Well, anyway, during our visit I found myself studying this most interesting religious woman, Mrs. Evermore. So religious and yet so—I don't even

27

know what to call her! And I don't want to misjudge her, but you asked me when I came to see the distinction between thoughts and things—"

"Yes, yes, no fear of my thinking ill of you for speaking honestly of her. Go on, my dear."

"From morning to night she was evermore on the hunt after new fancies—ideas, tiny tidbits of wisdom, well-worded phrases."

"She did seem to listen to everything we said as if she was always waiting for something," reflected Mr. Colman.

"For thoughts, sentiments, little poetic gems of insight! She watched for them, stalked them, followed them like a boy with a butterfly net. She caught them plentifully too. But none ever came to anything, so far as I could see. She never did anything with one of them. Whatever she caught had a cage to itself where she kept it to look at. Every other moment, while you and Mr. Dobson were talking, she would cry 'oh! oh! O—o—oh!' and pull out her notebook, which was the cork box in which she pinned her butterflies. She must have had a whole museum of ideas! The most accidental resemblance between words would suffice to start one: after it she would go, catch it, pin it down into her notebook, and think she had captured the meaning either you or Mr. Dobson intended. Now and then a very pretty notion would fall to her net, and often a silly one. But all were equally game to her.

"I found her amusing and interesting for two days, but then began to see she led nothing to nowhere. She was touchy and jealous and self-absorbed, and she said things that disgusted me. She never did anything for anybody else, and though she hunted religious ideas most, she never seemed to imagine they could have anything to do with her life. It was only the fineness of a good thought that she seemed to prize. She would startle you any moment by an exclamation of delight at some spiritual fancy or sentimentality, and down it must go in her book. But it went no further than her book. She was just the same as before—common, occasionally vulgar, selfish in her judgments and motives and actions, in no way such that anyone would look at her and think she was trying to live pleasing to her Father.

"In appearance she was a refined woman, but she took no trouble to be what she was made for. You have always told me, you know, that God makes us, but *we* have to be. Yet Mrs. Evermore seemed taking no trouble to be anything. She talked about afflictions as one might of manure, having no idea that by her afflictions, of which she would complain bitterly, she was being fashioned for life eternal.

"It was all the most dreary, noisome rubbish I had ever come across. I found myself lying awake after that, thinking what might be able to ever rouse such a woman to see that she had to *do* something, to see that neither man nor woman can become anything without having had a hand in the matter. She seemed to expect the spirit of God to work in her like yeast in flour, although there was not a sign of the dough rising.

"And that, Father, is how I came to see that one may have any number of fine thoughts and fancies, as high and spiritual as you please, and be nothing the better, any more than the poor woman in the gospel with all her doctors. And when Walter, the next time he came home, talked as he did about thoughts and quoted Keats to the same effect, as if the finest thing in the universe were a fine thought, I could not bear it; and that is what prompted me to speak to him as I did."

"You have made it very clear, Molly, and I quite agree with you. Thinks are of no use except they be turned into things."

"But perhaps, after all, I may have been unfair to Mrs. Evermore," said Molly. "People are so interesting! Sometimes they seem to be completely made up of odd bits of different people. Take Aunt Ann now! She wouldn't do a shopkeeper out of so much as a halfpenny, yet she will cheat at backgammon."

"I know she will, and that is why I never play with her. It is so seldom she will allow herself any recreation that it makes me sorry to refuse her."

"There is one thing that troubles me," said Molly after a pause.

"What is it, my child?"

"Are you sure you don't mind?"

"I always like to hear anything that is troubling you, for then I know you are about to have a new revelation. To wonder about something is the preparation for receiving more light."

"Well it's just this, then—I can't make myself care that much for poetry, yet Walter says such fine things about it. And Walter is no fool!"

"Far from one, I am glad to think!" replied his father, laughing. Molly's straightforward, humble confidence he found as delightful as amusing.

"It has always seemed silly to me to scoff at things because you don't happen to care for them or don't choose to go in for them. I sometimes hear people make offhand or derogatory remarks about music, and yet I know music is a good and precious and lovely thing. Then I think to myself that they must be in the same condition with regard to music that I am with regard to poetry. So I am careful not to be a fool in talking about what I don't know. That I am stupid about poetry is no reason for being a fool. Anyone whom God has made stupid has a right to be stupid. But no one has a right to call another a fool because that person has different tastes than he himself does."

"I thought you liked poetry, Molly."

"I do when you read it, or talk about it. You are always able to make your impression of it grow my way of understanding it deeper. I hear the poetry and feel your feeling of it. But when I try to read it myself, then I don't care much for it. Sometimes I turn it into prose, and then I can get hold of it better."

"That is about the best and hardest test you could put to it, Molly. But perhaps you have been trying to like what ought not to be liked."

"You mean I shouldn't like poetry?"

"I mean perhaps you shouldn't like *bad* poetry. Some of it does not deserve to be liked. There is much in the shape of poetry that set in gold and diamonds would be worth nothing."

"I don't know. I think rather that the difficulty is in myself. Sometimes I am in a mood fit for it, and other times not. A single line will now and then set something churning in me. It will make me think of music and sunrises and wind and the song of the lark, and all lovely things. But sometimes prose will serve me the same. And the next minute, perhaps, either of them will bore me more than I can bear. The difference must be something in me!"

"That may sometimes be, but certainly not always. You are fastidious, little one, and in exquisite things, how can one be too fastidious? When Walter is gone, suppose we read a little more poetry together?"

4 / Liberating Fatherhood

There are parents, even though they have found possession powerless for their own peace, who nonetheless seek to heap up things and wealth for the sons and daughters coming after them, in the weak but unquestioned fancy that possession and earthly gain will do for them what it could not do for their fathers and mothers.

Richard Colman was above such stupidity. He had indeed made some money during one of the good farming times, but had lately not been seeking to increase his holdings nor his wealth. He was a man too genuinely practical to set his mind upon making money. He had early come to see that the best thing money could do for his son was to help in preparing him for some work fit to employ what faculty had been given him, in accordance with the tastes also given him. He saw the last thing a foolish father will see: that the best a father can do is to enable his son to earn his livelihood in the exercise of a genial and righteous labor. He saw that possession generates artificial and enfeebling wants, overlaying and smothering the God-given necessities of our nature, from which alone can come golden hopes and manly endeavors.

Richard had therefore been in no hurry to push his son toward a choice of profession. When every man shall feel in himself a call to this or that, he scarcely needs to make a choice at all, for he feels compelled to follow that call, and thus will the generations be well served. But that time had not yet come in Walter's life, and what he was fit for was not yet quite clear. It was only clear to the father that his son must labor for others with a labor, if possible, whose reflex action should be life to himself. Following his own footsteps into a farming life seemed inadequate to the full employment of the mental gifts which, whether from paternal partiality or genuine insight, he believed his son to possess. Neither had Walter shown inclination or aptitude for any particular branch of agriculture. All Richard could do, therefore, was to give him such schooling and preparation as would be fundamentally helpful for any superstructure he might later build upon it. The clergy interested neither father nor son; inside, Richard hoped he might turn to medicine or the law. Partly for financial reasons, he sent him to the University in Edinburgh.

There Walter neither distinguished nor disgraced himself, and developed no particular inclination to one more than another of the careers open to a young man of education. He read a good deal, however, and showed taste in literature. Indeed, he was regarded by his companions as an authority in its more imaginative ranges, and especially in matters belonging to verse, having an exceptionally fine ear for its vocal delicacies. This is one of the rarest of gifts; but rarity does not determine value, and Walter greatly overestimated its relative importance, and thus began to think more highly of himself than he ought. The consciousness of his possession of this talent, and his inability to perceive its relative insignificance, had a far more than reasonable share in finally turning Walter's thoughts to literature as a profession.

When his bent became apparent, it troubled his father a little. He knew that to gain the level of excellence at which labor a writer or poet could hope for the most meager livelihood required in most cases a severe struggle. And for such a diligent effort he doubted his son's capacity. He perceived in him none of the stoic strength that comes of a high ideal, and can encounter disappointment, even privation, without injury, and can persevere toward the lofty goal. Other and deeper dangers the good parent did not see. He comforted himself that even if things went no better than they were now, he at least had means to give his son a fair chance of discovering whether the career would suit him, and if so, support him financially long enough until he should begin to attain the material end of it with income of his own.

Long before Miss Hancock's attack upon his supposed indifference to his son's idleness, Mr. Colman had made up his mind to let Walter see how far he could go as a hopeful writer. The next day he told his son, to Walter's unspeakable delight, that he was ready to do what lay in his power to further his desire, and that he would give him what money he could to support his effort and hopefully sustain him until he was making an income of his own. His own earthly life was precious to him, he said, only for the sake of the children he must eventually leave; and when he saw his son busy, contented, and useful, then his life on earth would be fulfilled and he would gladly yield his hold upon it.

Walter's imagination took fire at the prospect of realizing all he had longed for but had always feared to subject to parental scrutiny. So little did he yet apprehend his father's love that he had never dreamed his father would actually fall in with his plans! And he was at once eager to go out into the great unfriendly world in the hope of being soon regarded by his peers as the possessor of certain gifts and literary faculties that had not yet been fully recognized. For as the conscience of many a man seems never to trouble him until the looks of his neighbors bring their consciences to bear upon his, so the mind of many a man seems never to satisfy him that he has a gift until other men grant his possession of it.

Nevertheless, around Walter the world broke at once into rare bloom. He became like a windy day in the house, vexing his aunt with his loud, foolish gladness, and causing the wise heart of Molly many a sudden and chilly foreboding. His father loved him and would do his best for him, and in that love would liberate him to discover what he could of himself. But Molly knew him better than his father. His father had not played with him day after day! Molly knew that happiness made him feel strong for anything, but that his happiness was easily dashed, and that he was then a rain-wet, wind-beaten butterfly. He had no soul for bad weather.

But he could not therefore be kept inside and protected forever. He must have his trial. He must, in one way or another, encounter life, and find out what amount of the real might be in him. He must discover what little, but enlargeable claim he might have to manhood!

5 / Walter Seeks His Fortune in the City_____

Not then even knowing half of what the words meant, Walter wrote the following little poem:

> Every morning, a man may say,
> Calls him up with a new birthday;
> Every day is a little life,
> Sunny with love, stormy with strife;
> Every night is a little death,
> From which too soon he awakeneth.

As with the skirt of her mantle the dark of the sunset wipes out the day, so with her sleep, the night makes a man fresh for the new day's journey. If it were not for sleep, the world could not go on. To feel the mystery of day and night, to gaze into the far receding spaces of their marvel, is more than to know all the facts of science and all the combinations of chemistry. A little wonder is worth tons of knowledge in truly *knowing* what the universe means.

But to Walter the new day did not come as a call to new life in the world of will and action, but only as the harbinger of bliss borne hitherward on the wind of the world. Was he not going forth as a Titanic child to become a great man among great men! Would he not become one of the strong among the weak! Would he not be great among the small!

He did not suspect in himself what Molly saw, or at least suspected in him. He was too enamored with the idea of becoming great to give heed to becoming true.

When a man is hopeful, he feels strong and can work. The thoughts come and the pen runs. Were he always at his best, what might not a man do! Even the least of men, when they are at their best, can accomplish wonderful things.

But not many can determine their moods. And none—be they poets or economists, teachers or novelists, or businessmen—can guarantee they will always have an energetic and fertile condition of mind any more than they can create their minds in the first place. When the mood changes and hope departs, and the inward atmosphere grows damp and dismal, there may be some whose imagination and energy will yet respond to their call. But yet if some certain kind of illness come, eventually every man must lose his power—both physical and mental. His creature condition will assert itself. He is compelled to discover that we did not create ourselves; neither do we live by ourselves.

Walter loved his father, but did not mind leaving him. He loved Molly, but did not mind leaving her. And we cannot blame him if he was glad to escape from his aunt. If people are not lovable, it takes a saint to love them, or at least one who is not afraid of them. Yet it was with a sense of somewhat dreary though welcome liberty that Walter found himself, all except for his friend, the young man his father had befriended, alone in London. With his help Walter found a humble lodging not far from the British Museum, to the neighborhood of which his love of books led him. And for a time, feeling no urgent necessity for immediate effort, he gave himself to the reading and study at the museum of certain departments of our English not before within his easy reach. In the evening he would write, or accompany his friend to some lecture or amusement. And so the weeks passed.

To earn something seemed but a slowly approaching necessity, and the weeks grew to months. He was never idle, for his tastes were strong, and he had delight in his pen. But so sensitive was his social skin, partly from the licking of his aunt's dry feline tongue, and so greatly was he afraid of potential criticism, that he shrank from submitting anything he wrote to his friend Harold Sullivan, who, made of firmer and more world-capable stuff than Walter, would at least have shown him how things that the author saw and judged from the inner side of the web must appear on the other side. There are few weavers of thought capable of turning round the web and contemplating with unprejudiced regard the side of it about to be offered to the world, so as to perceive how it will look to eyes alien to its maker.

It would be to repeat a story often told, to relate how he sent poem after poem, now to this, now to that magazine, with the same result each time—that he never heard of them again. The verses over which he had labored with delight, in the crimson glory they reflected on the heart whence they issued, were nothing in any eyes to which he submitted them.

In truth, except for a good line here and there, they were by no means on the outer side what they looked to him on the inner. He read them in the light of the feeling in which he had written them; whoever else read them did not have this light to interpret them by, and had no similar mood ready to receive them. It was the business of the verse itself, by witchery of sound and magic of phrase, to rouse receptive mood in the mind of the reader—of this level of poetry poor Walter was incapable.

A course of reading in the first attempts of such of our country's poets who eventually rose to well-merited distinction might have revealed to him many helpful things—among the rest, their frequent poverty and the newness of the ideas they put forth, though it often took years before it was recognized. Much mere babbling often issues before worthy speech begins. But Walter was not cognizant of such truths. His babbling was not leading toward worthy speech, for in himself he had nothing to say. There was nothing in his mind to be put in form except a few of the vague lovely sensations belonging to a poetic temperament.

And as he grew more and more of a reader, his inspiration came more and more from what he read, less and less from knowledge of his own heart, or even the hearts of others. He had no revelation to give. He had, like far too many of our preachers, set out to run before he could walk, begun to cry aloud before he had any truth to utter, attempted to teach, or at least interest others, before he himself was interested in others. Now and then, indeed, especially when some fading joy of childhood gleamed up in his brain out of the past, words could come unbidden, and he would quickly dash out a song or poem which showed true feeling and music. But this kind of thing he scarcely valued, for it seemed to cost him nothing.

He comforted himself by concluding that his work was of a kind too original to be at once recognized by dulled and sated editors, and that he must labor on and keep sending.

"Why do you not write something for publication?" his friend would say, to whom Walter had not made known either his efforts or his rejections. He would answer that his time was not come.

The friends he made were not many. To his credit he did not sink into low ways, but maintained his integrity. Instinctively he shrank from what was coarse, feeling it destructive to every finer element. How could he write of beauty if he turned but for a moment to the unclean and was thus false to beauty? But he was far from satisfied with himself: he had done nothing, even in his own eyes, so long as the recognition of the world was lacking!

He was in no anxiety, for he did not imagine it mattering to his father whether he began a little sooner or a little later to earn his own way. There was plenty for him to live on for a long time. His father knew, he said to himself, that to earn money ought not to be a man's first object in life, even when necessity compelled him to make it first in order of time, which was not the case with him!

But he did not ask himself whether he had substituted a better object in place of the lesser. A greater man than himself, he reflected—no less a man, indeed, than Milton—had never earned so much as a dinner until after he was thirty years of age! He did not consider how and to what ends Milton had all the time been diligent. Walter was no student yet of men's lives. He was interested almost only in their imaginations, and not half fastidious enough as to whether those imaginations ran upon the rails of truth or not. He was rapidly filling his mind with the good and bad of the literature of his country, but he had not yet gone far in distinguishing between the bad and the good in it. Books were to him the geological deposits of literary forces. He pursued his acquaintance with them to nourish the literary faculty in himself. They afforded him atmosphere and stimulant, as well as a store of ideas. He was in full training for the profession that cultivates literature for and upon literature, and neither for nor upon truth.

6 / A Sudden Change

A big stone fell suddenly into the smooth pool of Walter's conditions. A letter from his father brought the news that the bank where he had deposited his savings had proved but a swollen mushroom. He had lost everything.

"Indeed, my son," wrote the sorrowful Mr. Colman, "I do not honestly see how I can send you another shilling. If you have exhausted the proceeds of my last check and can not earn sufficiently to keep you going, come home. My roof at least is yours still. Thank God, the land yet remains!—so long as I can pay the rent."

A new impulse awoke in the heart of Walter as a result. He drew himself up for combat and endurance. I am afraid he did not feel much sadness over his father's trouble, but he would have scorned adding to it by increasing his father's financial burden. He wrote at once, telling him he must not worry about him at all; he would do very well. It was not a comforting letter exactly, but it showed courage, and his father was glad.

Walter thereupon set himself to find work. If his creativity could not yet pay his way, perhaps he might find employment instead in some one of the mechanical departments of literature. For literature was still his field—the only region in which he could think to do anything—and if he could not create the written word out of his head, perhaps he might dispense it with his hand.

When the architect comes to necessity, it is good if stones are near—and the mason's hammer. If he be not the better mason because he is an architect, alas for his architecture! If the author, driven by necessity to the presses and binding machines of the publishing house, cannot make better books because he also writes them, then what can be said for his love for the printed word? He who most deeply loves the designs of a building and the ideas of a book will be the one who cares most strongly to see that building and that book made with such distinction as suits the creative image.

Walter was nothing yet, however—neither architect nor stone-mason, neither author nor bookbinding craftsman—when the stern hand of financial necessity laid hold of him. But it is a fine thing for any man to be compelled to work. It is the first divine decree, issuing from love and help. How would it have been with Adam and Eve had they been left only to plenty and idleness, the voice of God no more heard in the cool of the day?

But the search for work was a difficult and disheartening task. He who has encountered it, however, has had an experience whose value far more than equals its unpleasantness. A man out of work needs the God that cares for the sparrows as much as the man whose heart is torn with ingratitude, or crushed under a secret crime.

Walter went here and there, and made his need for work known to his few acquaintances. He obtained some introductions, and even without any went to some who might have employment to offer, putting so much pride in his pockets that had his vainglory been solid, the pockets would have bulged in unsightly fashion. Thus he walked about the city till worn with weariness, giving good proof that he was no fool but had the right stuff deep within him. He neither yielded to false fastidiousness, nor relaxed his effort because of disappointment—not even when disappointment became the very atmosphere of his consciousness. To the father it would have been heartache indeed to see his son wiping the sweat and dust from the forehead his mother had been so affectionately proud of, and to hear the heavy sigh with which he would sink in the not-too-easy chair that was his only haven after the day's weary search. He did not rise quite above self-pity; he thought indeed that he was being harshly dealt with by life. But so long as he did not respond to the foolish and weakening sentiment by relaxation of effort, it could not do him much harm. He would soon grow out of it and learn to despise it.

What one man has borne, why should not another bear? Why should it be unfit for him any more than the other? Certainly he who has never borne has yet to bear. The new experience is awaiting every member of the Dives clan. Walter wore out his shoes and could not buy another pair. His clothes grew shabby, and he had no choice but to go on wearing them. It was no small part of his suffering to have to show himself in a guise that made him look so different from the man he felt he was. But he did not let his father know even a small part of the misery he faced.

He had never drawn close to his father; they had come to no spiritual contact. The son had never opened his eyes to truly see the father. Walter the gentleman saw in Richard Colman only the farmer. He knew him to be an honorable man, and in a small way could be said to honor him. But he would have been dissatisfied with him in such society to which he considered himself belonging. It is a sore thing for a father when he has shoved his son up a steep craggy incline only to see him walk away the moment he reached the top without looking behind. Walter felt a difference between them—in a word, thought he had advanced further in society, therefore was "better" than his father.

Finally he could no longer pay the rent and had to give up his lodging. Sullivan took him into his and shared what he had with him—doing all he could in return for Richard Colman's kindness.

Where was Walter's poetry now? Naturally, vanished. He was man enough to work, but not man enough to continue as a poet. There was scarcely anything of real poetry within him! Indeed, how could such a jade stand the spur!

But to stir himself to action was a better thing than to make verses, and indeed of all the labors for a livelihood in which a man may cultivate verse, that of literature is the last he should choose. Compare the literary efforts of Burns late in life with the songs he wrote as a farmer when home from the plough!

In truth, Walter's hope of ever finding a job had begun to faint outright as he lay on the floor one evening when Sullivan came in and told him that the editor of a new periodical, whom Harold had met at a friend's house, would make a place for young Colman. The pay could only suffice to scratch out the merest income, but at least it would mean bread. More, it was work, and a potential opening to possibilities. Walter felt himself up to enduring anything short of weakening hunger, and gladly accepted the offer. His duties were but an agglomeration of menial tasks, but even in that he might show faculty, and who could tell what might follow. It was wearisome but not altogether arduous, and above all, it still left him with time for himself.

7 / An Opening

Walter found that compulsory employment, while taking from his time for genial labor of choice, at the moment quickened his desire after it once more, increased his faculty for it, and made him more careful of his precious hours of leisure. Life, too, now took on a greater interest than before; and almost as soon as anxiety over the daily necessities passed, the impulse to utterance began again to urge him.

What this impulse is, who can define, or who can trace its origin? The result of it in Walter's case was ordered words, or poetry. Seldom is such a result of any value, but the process for the man is invaluable. It remained to be seen whether in Walter it was for others as well as himself.

He became rapidly capable of better work. His duty at the magazine was drudgery, but drudgery well encountered will reveal itself as of potent and precious reaction, both intellectual and moral. One incapable of drudgery cannot be capable of the finest work. Many a man may do many things well, and be far from reception into the most ancient guild of workers.

Walter labored with conscience and diligence, and brought his good taste to tell on the quality of his drudgery. The work did him good, and he did the work well. He is a contemptible workman who thinks of his claims before his duties, and of his poor wages instead of his undertaken work. He who works merely for the return to be paid him will never be the best worker, nor will the work benefit him as honest labor was intended to do. There was a strong sense of fairness in Walter. He saw the dishonesty of pocketing even the most meager wages without giving good work in return. That he believes himself capable of higher work is the worst of reasons for a man not giving money's worth for the money he receives. That a certain piece of work may be of little value in his eyes is a poor excuse for giving bad measure of it. Walter carried his hod full, and was thus closer to being a man than at any previous time in his life.

Sullivan was mainly employed by a certain literary journal in London, writing reviews of current literature. One evening he brought Walter a book of some pretension, told him he was behind with his work, and begged him to write a notice about it. Glad for the opportunity both to serve his friend and to try his own hand, Walter started reading the book at once. The moment he thus took the attitude of a reviewer, he found the paragraphs begin, like potatoes, to sprout, and generate other paragraphs. Between agreeing and disagreeing, he soon had far more than enough to say. He got up and went to the table, as a workman his bench.

To many people, writing is the greatest of bores. But Walter enjoyed it, even the mechanical part of the operation. Paying no attention to the length of his article, he wrote until long after midnight, and the next morning handed the result to his friend.

"Here's a paper for a quarterly!" Sullivan cried as he burst out laughing. "Man, it's almost as long as the book! This will never do! The world has neither time, space, money, nor brains for so much. But I will take it and see what can be done with it."

The result was that about a sixth of it was printed. And in that sixth Walter could not even recognize his own hand, neither could he have gathered from it any idea of what the book was about. There it was, however, and to see something—anything!—with which he had a hand, however small, in writing sent a certain electrical thrill through his brain.

A few days later, Harold brought him a batch of books to review, taking care, however, to limit him to an average length for each. Walter entered thus upon a short apprenticeship during the evening hours, the end of which was that when a vacancy happened to occur on the staff of the journal, he was offered the position. He therewith terminated his tedious job, and within two weeks was placed "on the staff" to aid in reviewing the books sent in by publishers. His income was considerably increased, but the work was more demanding, and required more of his time.

From the very first he was troubled to find how much more honesty demanded than pay made possible. He had not learned this while merely supplementing the labor of his friend and taking his time. But now he became aware that to make acquaintance with a book, and pass upon it a justifiable judgment, required at least four times the attention he could afford to give it, paid as he was by the review, and live. On the other hand, many reviews he could knock off without compunction, regarding them as too slight to deserve attention. Indifferently honest, he was not so sensitive in justice as to reflect that the poorest thing has a right to fair play, that, free to say nothing, you must, if you speak, say the truth even of the lowest thing. But Walter had not yet sunk so low as to believe there can be necessity for doing wrong. The world is divided, very unequally, into those who think a man cannot avoid, and those who believe he must avoid doing wrong. The former live in fear of death, the latter set death in one eye and right in the other.

His first important review, Walter was compelled to print without having finished it. The next he worked at harder, and finished, but with less deliberation. He grew more and more careless toward the books he counted of little consequence, while he imagined himself growing more and more capable of getting at the heart of a book by skimming its pages. If to skim be ever a true faculty, it must come of long experience in the art of reading, and is not possible to a beginner. To skim and judge is to wake from a doze and give the charge to a jury.

With practice, his prose improved and indeed grew crisp. But writing more and more smartly, he found the usual difficulty in abstaining from a smartness that was unjust because irrelevant.

So far as his employers were concerned, Walter did his duty. But he forgot that, apart from his obligation to the mere and paramount truth, it was from the books he reviewed—good, bad, or indifferent, whichever they were—that he drew the food he ate and the clothes that covered him. He began to think too highly of himself as "original," as he had once foolishly thought about his poetry, a condition made all the worse that he did begin to exhibit some genuine proficiency for writing.

His talent was increasingly recognized by the editors of the newspaper, and they began to put other, and what they counted more important work, in front of him to do, entrusting him with the editorial discussion of certain social questions of the day, regarding which, like many of small experience, he found it the easier to give a confident opinion in that his experience was so small. In general he wrote logically, and, which is rarer, was even capable of being made to see where his logic was wrong. But his premises were much too scanty. What he took for granted was very often by no means granted.

None of this mattered, however, to the editors and owners of the paper, so long as he wrote lucidly, sparklingly, cleverly. His pieces, therefore, left those who read them, concerning the depth of whose reading it would perhaps be revealing to inquire, willing to read more and more from the same pen.

8 / Flattery

Within a year Walter began to be known—to the profession, at least—as a promising young writer. He was already personally known to a growing number within the literary circles as a very agreeable, gentlemanly fellow, so that in the following social season he had a good many invitations to an array of gatherings and functions. It was by nothing beyond the transitory that he was known, but may not the man who has invented a good umbrella one day build a good palace?

His acquaintance was considerably varied, but of the social terraces above the professional he knew nothing for a time.

One evening, however, he happened to meet, and was presented to a certain Lady Tremaine. She had asked to have the refined-looking young man, of whom she had just heard as one of the principal writers in the *Field Battery,* introduced to her. She was a matronly, handsome woman, with cordial manners and a cold eye—frank, easy, confident, unassuming. Under the shield of her nobility, she would walk straight up to any subject and speak her mind of it plainly. It was more than easy to become acquainted with her when she chose.

The company was not a large one, and they soon found themselves alone in a quiet corner.

"You are a celebrated literary man, they tell me, Mr. Colman," said Lady Tremaine.

"Not in the least," answered Walter. "I am but a poor hack."

"It is good to be modest. But I am not bound to take your description of yourself. Professionals are, I should think, in a fair position to take the lead—especially writers."

"In what way?"

"In politics, in society, in everything."

"Your ladyship cannot think such a thing desirable?"

"I do not pretend to desire seeing the professional class sup-
plant those of traditional position. I will not be false to my own
people. But the fact remains that in these times of change, people
such as yourself are coming to the front, and we of the nobility
are falling behind. And the sooner you get to the front, the better
it will be for the world, and for us too."

"I cannot say I understand you."

"I will tell you why. There are now no fewer than three aristocracies—one of rank, and one of brains. I belong to the one,
you to the other. But there is a third."

"If you recognize the rich as an aristocracy, you must allow
me to differ most strongly with you."

"Naturally. I quite agree with you. But what can your opinion
and mine avail against the rising popular tide? All the old families
of both wealth and position are melting away, swallowed by the
nouveau riche. I should not mind, or at least I should feel it in
me to submit with a good grace, if we were pushed from our
stools by a new aristocracy of literature and science. But I do
rebel against the social *regime* that is every day more strongly
asserting itself. All the gradations are fast disappearing. The pal-
isades of good manners, dignity, and respect are vanishing with
the hedges. The country is positively inundated with slang and
vulgarity—all from the ill-breeding, presumption, and self-
satisfaction of new people."

She paused, but Walter did not reply immediately, and she
resumed.

"The best, and indeed the only thing to help, is that the two
other aristocracies make common cause and join together in keeping the rich in their proper place."

It was not a very subtle flattery, but Walter was pleased. The
lady saw she had so far gained her end, for she was one who
always had a design in what she said, and changed the subject.

"You go out evenings, I see," she said at length. "I am glad.
Some authors will not."

"I do when I can. The evening, however, to one who—who—"

"Of course! I see your hesitation. How silly all our pursuits, with their gold and diamonds, must appear in your eyes! But I hope you will make an exception in my favor."

"I shall be happy to," replied Walter cordially.

"I will not ask you to come and be absorbed in a crowd—not the first time at least! Could you not manage to come to see me in the morning?"

"I am at your service," replied Walter.

"Then come—let me see—the day after tomorrow—shall we make it the afternoon instead?—say, about five o'clock—17, Goodrich square."

Walter could not but be flattered that Lady Tremaine was so evidently pleased with him. She called his profession an aristocracy too. Therefore, she did not seem to be patronizing him, but almost receiving him on the same social level as herself! We cannot blame him for the inexperience that allowed him to hold his head a little higher as he walked home.

There was little danger of his forgetting the appointment. Lady Tremaine received him in the room she called her "growlery," with cordiality. By and by she led the talk toward literature.

"We are not in this house altogether ignorant of your profession," she said after they had talked briefly of several new books. "My daughter Lufa is an authoress in her own way. You, of course, would never have heard of her. But her volume of verse came out just twelve months ago."

Quickly Walter racked his brain. Surely when helping his friend Sullivan somewhere about that time, he had seen a small ornate volume of verses, with a strange name like that on the title page! Whether he had written a notice of it he could not remember.

"It was exceedingly well received—for a first effort, of course! Lufa hardly thought so herself, but I told her it was the best she could hope to expect, altogether unknown as she was. Tell me honestly, Mr. Colman, is there not quite as much jealousy in the writing profession as in any other?"

Walter replied, allowing that it was not immaculate with respect to envy and speaking down upon others.

"You yourself, as a reviewer and critic, have so much opportunity for revenge," said Lady Tremaine. "And such a coat of darkness for protection! With a few strokes of the pen, a man in your position may ruin his rival!"

"Scarcely that!" returned Walter. "If a book be a good book, the worst of us cannot do it much harm. Nor do I believe there are more than a few in the profession who would condescend to give a false opinion upon the work of a rival. To be a writer in the first place implies a certain interest in truth, one would think, though doubtless personal feeling may pervert the judgment."

"That, of course," returned the lady, "is but human. However, you cannot deny that authors occasionally make furious assaults on each other."

"Authors ought not to be reviewers," replied Walter. "I imagine most reviewers avoid even the work of an acquaintance, not to say a friend or an enemy."

The door opened, and what seemed to Walter as lovely a face as could ever have dawned on the world peeped in and would have withdrawn.

"Lufa," said Lady Tremaine, "you need not go away. Come in and be introduced to Mr. Colman."

She entered—a small, pale creature, below average height, with the daintiest figure, and childlike eyes of dark blue, very clear and wide. Her hair was brown, on the side of black, divided in the middle and gathered behind in a great mass. Her dress was something white, with a shimmer of red about it, and a blush-rose in the front.

She greeted Walter in the simplest, friendliest way, holding out her tiny hand very frankly. Her features were no smaller than for her size they ought to have been, perfect in themselves, Walter thought, and in harmony with her whole being and carriage. Her manner was a gentle, unassuming assurance—almost as if they knew each other but had not met for some time. Walter felt some ancient primeval bond between them—dim, but unmistakable.

The mother withdrew to her writing table and began to write, now and then throwing in a word as they talked. Lady Lufa seemed pleased with her new acquaintance. Walter was altogether bewitched. Bewitchment I take to be the approach of the real to our ideal. Perhaps upon that, however, depends even the comforting or the restful. In the heart of everyone lies the necessity for homeliest interaction with the perfectly lovely; we are made for it. Yet we are so far from the ideal in ourselves, an ideal which no man can come near until absolutely devoted to its quest, that we continually take that for sufficing which is only a little beyond our vision, but nowhere close to the *true* ideal.

"I think, Mr. Colman, I have seen something of yours!—You do put your name to what you write?" said Lady Lufa.

"Not always," replied Walter. "I am sure the poem must have been yours!"

It so happened that Walter had just then for the first time published a thing of his own. That it should have arrested the eye of this lovely creature was almost too good to be true! He acknowledged that he had printed a trifle in *The Observatory*.

"I was *charmed* with it!" said the girl, the word charmingly drawn out.

"The merest trifle," remarked Walter. "It cost me scarcely a thought." He meant what he said, unwilling to be judged by such a slight thing.

"That is the beauty of it!" she answered. "Your poem left your soul as the thrush's song leaves his throat."

Walter laughed. "But we are not meant to sing like the birds."

"That you could write such a song without effort shows that you possess the bird-gift of spontaneity."

Walter was surprised at her talk, and willing to believe it profound.

"The will and the deed in one may be the highest art," he said. "I hardly know."

"May I write music to your verses?" asked Lady Lufa, with an upward glance, sweet smile, and gently apologetic look.

"I am delighted you should think of doing so. It is more than it deserves!" answered Walter. "My only condition is that you will let me hear it."

"That you certainly have a right to. Besides, I would dare not publish it without knowing you liked it."

"Thank you. To hear you sing it will let me know at once whether the song itself be genuine."

"No, no! I may fail in my part, and yours still be everything I said it was. But I shall not fail. Your poem has taken hold on me too strongly for that."

"Then I may hope for an invitation to hear it," said Walter, rising.

"Before long. But one cannot order the mood, you know!"

9 / The Round of the World

When they leave the nest, birds, I presume, carry their hearts with them. Not a few humans leave their hearts behind them—too often, alas! to be sent for afterward. The whole round of the world, many a drifting mass of clouds, and many a mist on the top of that, rises between them and the eyes and hearts which gave their very life that they might live.

Some as they approach middle age, some only when they are old, wake up to understand that they have parents. To some the perception comes with their children. To others the realization hits with the pang of seeing their own sons and daughters walk away lighthearted out into the world, as they themselves turned their backs on their parents: they had been all their own, and now they have done with them. Less or more have we not all thus taken our journey into a far country?

But many a man of sixty is more of a son to the father gone from the earth than he was while under his roof. What a disintegrated mass would the world be, what a lump of half-baked brick, if death were indeed the end of love! if there were no more chance of setting right what was so wrong in the loveliest relations! How gladly would many a son who once thought it a weariness to serve his parents minister now to their lightest need! And in the boundless eternity shall we think there is no help?

Walter was not exactly a prodigal; he was a well-behaved youth with certain external scruples, and even a good many external characteristics many a father might even be proud of. His shortcomings would have been considered slight indeed by the world. He was *only* proud, after all, and how great a sin can that be? He was not hypocritical, *only* a little pharisaical, *only* thought too much of himself, was *only* neglectful of those nearest him, but always polite to those comparatively nothing to him. Small *onlys,* these does my reader say. Compassionate and generous to necessity, he let his father and his adoptive sister starve for the only real food a man can give, that is, himself. As to Him who thought his very thoughts into him, Walter heeded him not at all, or mocked him—like a multitude of churchgoers, not knowing it was mockery—by merest religious ceremony. There are those who refuse God the drink of water he desires on the grounds that their vessel is not fit for him to drink from. Walter, on the other hand, thought his too good to fill with the water fit for God to drink.

He had the feeling, far from worded to himself, not even formed, but certainly in him, that he was a superior man to his father. But it is a fundamental necessity of the kingdom of heaven, impossible as it must seem to all outside it, that each shall count others better than himself. Such is the natural condition of the man and woman God made, in relation to the other men and women God has made. Man is made, not to contemplate himself, but to behold in others the beauty of the Father. A man who lives to meditate upon and worship himself is in the slime of hell. Walter knew his father was a reading man, but because the older man had not been to a university, the son placed no value on his father's reading. Yet Richard Colman was a man who had communion in the high countries, communion in which his son would not have perceived the presence of an idea.

In like manner, Richard Colman's carriage of mind and the expression of his mind-set (perhaps I should call it instead his heart-set) in his modes of behavior toward everyone with whom he had to do were no doubt pleasing to the ushers of those high countries. His was a certain, quiet, simple, direct way, reminding one of Nathanael, in whom was no guile. In another man Walter would have called it rustic, unrefined; in his father he shut his eyes to it as well as he could, and was ashamed of it. He would scarcely, in *his* circle, be regarded as a gentleman! He would look and sound odd! The country would hang too obviously about him!

Walter had therefore not encouraged the idea of his father coming to see him. He was not satisfied with the father by whom the Father of fathers had sent him into the world. But Mr. Colman was the truest of gentlemen even in his outward carriage, for he was not only courteous and humble, but also that rare thing— natural. And the natural, be it old as the Greek, must be beautiful. The natural dwells deep, and is not the careless, any more than the studied or assumed.

It could be said that Walter loved his father. But the root of his love did not go deep enough to send aloft a fine flower: deep in is high out. He seldom wrote home, and when he did he wrote briefly. He did not make a confidant of his father into his affairs. He did not even tell the man what his son was doing, or what he hoped to do. He would mention a small success now and then; but of hopes, fears, aspirations, or defeats, of thoughts or desires, he said nothing. As to his ideas and beliefs and theories, he never imagined his father entering into such things as occupied *his* mind! The ordinary young man takes it for granted that he and the world are far ahead of the earthly father under whose care he grew able to first see the world at all. Yet more often than such youths can comprehend, their fathers may have left behind them, as nebulae sinking below the horizon of youth itself, questions the world is but just waking to ask itself.

The blame, however, may lie in part at the parent's door. The hearts of the fathers need turning to the children as much as the hearts of the children need turning to the fathers. Few men open up to their children. And where a man does not, the schism, the separation begins with him. Even if his love for his son or daughter be deep and true, without opening, without communication between heart and heart, there will eventually come such division. That it is unmanly to show one's feelings is an untrue superstition prevalent with all English-speaking people. Now wherever feeling means weakness, falsehood, or mere temporary excitement, perhaps they ought not to be shown. But for a man to hide from his son his true feelings, his loving and his loathing, is to refuse him the divinest fashion of teaching.

Mr. Colman read the best things, and loved the best writers. Yet never once had he read a poem with his son, talked to him about any poet, or searched the Scriptures with him for their meaning. If Walter had even suspected his father's insight into certain things, he would have loved him more. Closely bound as they were, neither knew the other. Each would have been astonished at what he found in the other. The father might have discovered many handles by which to lay hold of his son. And the son might have seen the lamp bright in his father's chamber that he was still but trimming in his.

10 / The Song and Where It Led_____

At length came the summons from Lady Lufa to hear her music to his verses. It was not much of a poem:

Mist and vapour and cloud
    Filled the earth and the air!
My heart was wrapt in a shroud,
    And death was everywhere.

The sun went silently down
    To his rest in the unseen wave;
But my heart, in its purple and crown,
    Lay already in its grave.

For a cloud had darkened the brow
    Of the lady who is my queen;
I had been a monarch, but now
    All things had only been!

I sprang from the couch of death
    Who called my soul? Who spake?
No sound! no answer! no breath!
    Yet my soul was wide awake!

And my heart began to blunder
    Into rhythmic pulse the while;
I turned—away was the wonder—
    My queen had begun to smile!

Outbrake the sun in the west!
    Outlaughed the crested sea!
And my heart was alive in my breast
    With light, and love, and thee!

There was a bit of a lilt to the verses, and they had a meaning—though not a very new or valuable one.

He went in the morning, was shown into the drawing room, his heart beating with expectation. Lady Lufa was alone and already at the piano. She wore a gray worsted garment with red rosebuds, and looked as simple as any country parson's daughter. She gave him no greeting beyond a little nod, at once struck a chord or two, and began to sing.

Walter was charmed. The singing, and the song that emerged through the singing, altogether exceeded his expectation. He had been afraid he should not be able to laud it heartily, for he had not lost his desire to be truthful—but she was an artist! There was indeed nothing original in her music. It was mainly a reconstruction of common phrases afloat in the musical atmosphere. But she managed the slight dramatic element in the lyric with taste and skill, following tone and sentiment with chord and inflection, so that the music was worthy of the verses—which is not saying very much for either—while the expression the girl threw into the song went to the heart of the youth, and made him foolish.

She ceased. He was silent for a moment, then fervent in thanks and admiration.

"The verses are mine no more," he said. "I shall care for them now!"

"You won't mind if I publish them with the music?"

"I shall feel more honored than I dare tell you. But how am I to go to my work after this taste of paradise! It was too cruel of you, Lady Lufa, to make me come in the morning!"

"I am very sorry."

"Will you grant me one favor to make it up?"

"Yes."

"Never to sing the song to anyone when I am present. I could not bear it."

"I promise," she answered, looking up in his face with a glance of sympathetic consciousness.

At once there was an acknowledged secret between them, and Walter hugged it. "I gave you a frozen bird," he said, "and you have warmed it, and made it soar and sing."

"Thank you—a very pretty compliment!" she answered—and there was a moment's silence.

"I am so glad we know each other," she resumed. "You could

help me so much if you would! Next time you come, you must tell me something about those old French rhymes that have come into fashion lately! They say a pretty thing so much more prettily for their quaint, antique, courtly liberty. The triolet now—how deliciously impertinent it is—is it not!"

Walter knew nothing about the old French methods of verse, and, unwilling to place himself at a disadvantage, made an evasive reply, then rose and left.

But when at length he reached home, it was with several old volumes, among the rest *Clement Marot,* in pockets and hands. Before an hour was over, he was in delight with the variety of dainty modes in which, by shape and sound, a very pretty French something was carved out of nothing at all. Their fantastic surprises, the ring of their bell-like returns upon themselves, their music of triangle and cymbal gave him quite a new pleasure. In some of them poetry seemed to approach the nearest possible to bird-song—to unconscious seeming through most conscious art, imitating the carelessness and impromptu of warblings as old as the existence of birds and as new as every fresh individual joy. For each new generation grows its own feathers, and sings its own song, yet always the feathers of its kind and the song of its kind.

That same night he sent her the following *triolet*.

Oh, why is the moon
Awake when thou sleepest?
To the nightingale's tune,
Why is the moon
Making a noon,
When night is the deepest?
Why is the moon
Awake when thou sleepest?

That same evening came a little note, with a coronet on the paper, but neither date nor signature:

Perfectly delicious! How can such a little gem hold so much color? Thank you a thousand times!

By this, does my reader suppose Walter was in love with Lady

Lufa. He said as much to himself, at least. And in truth he was almost possessed with her. Every thought that rose in his mind began at once to drift toward her. Every hour of the day had a rose tinge from the dress in which he first saw her.

One might write a long essay on this thing called love, and yet contribute little to the understanding of it in the individual case. Its kind is to be interpreted after the kind of person who loves. There are as many hues and shades, not to say forms and constructions of love, as there are human countenances, human hearts, human judgments and schemes of life. Walter had not been an impressionable youth, because he had an imagination that made him discriminating and difficult to please. When a man can give form to the things that move in him, he is less driven to fall in love. But now Walter saw everything through a window, and that window was the face of Lufa. His thinking was always done in the presence and light of that window. She seemed an intrinsic component of every one of his mental operations. In every beauty and attraction of life he saw her. He was possessed by her, almost as some are by evil spirits. And to be possessed, even by a human being, may be to take refuge in the tombs, there to cry, and cut oneself with fierce thoughts.

But not yet was Walter troubled. He lived in love's eternal present, and did not look forward. Even jealousy had not yet begun to show itself in any shape. He was not in Lady Lufa's social set, and therefore not much drawn to conjecture what might be going on. In the glamour of literary ambition, he took for granted that Lady Lufa allotted his world a higher orbit than that of her social life, and prized most the pleasures they had in common, which so few were capable of sharing.

She had indeed in her own circle never found one who knew more of the refinements of verse than a schoolgirl does of Beethoven. And it was a great satisfaction to her to know one who not merely recognized her proficiency, but could guide her further into the depths of an art which everyone thinks he understands, and only one here and there truly does. It was therefore a real welcome she was able to give him when they met, as they did again and again during the social season. How much she cared for him, how much she would have been glad to do for him, my reader shall judge for himself. I think she cared for him very nearly as much as she would for a dress made to her liking. An injustice from him would have brought the tears into her eyes. A poem he disapproved of she would have thrown aside, perhaps into the fire.

She did not, however, submit much of her work to his judgment. She was afraid of what might put her out of heart with it. Before making his acquaintance, she had a new volume, a more ambitious one, well on its way to completion. But fearing lack of his praise, she had said nothing to him about it. And besides this diffidence, she did not wish to *appear* to solicit from him a good review. She might cast herself on his mercy, but it should not be confessedly. She had pride, though not conscience in the matter. The mother was capable of begging, but not the daughter. She might use fascination, but never would she entreat him to further her career; that would be to degrade herself!

Walter had, of course, taken a second look at her volume. It did not reveal that he had said of it what was not true. But he did see that had he been anxious to praise, he might have found passages to commend, or in which, at least, he could have pointed out merit. Though on the whole there was no change from his first impression. But no allusion was made to the book—on the one hand because Lady Lufa was aware he had written the review, and on the other because Walter did not wish to give his opinion of it. He placed it in the category of first works, and knowing how poor those of afterwards distinguished writers may be, it did not annoy him that one who could talk so well should have written such rubbish.

Lady Lufa possessed indeed a craze for composition, and the indulgence of it was encouraged by her faculty. There was no reason in heaven, earth, or the other place, why what she wrote should see the light, for it had little to do with light of any sort. Her first, entitled *Autumn Leaves*, had no such reception as her mother would have Walter believe. Lady Tremaine was one of those good mothers who, like so-called "good churchmen," will wrong any other to get something for their own. She had paid her court to Walter that she might gain a reviewer who would yield her daughter what she called justice: for justice' sake she would curry favor!

A half-merry, half-retaliative humor in Lufa may have wrought revenge by making Walter fall in love with her. At all events, it was a consolation to her wounded vanity when she saw him in love with her, but it was chiefly in the hope of a "good review" of her next book that she cultivated his acquaintance, and now she was beginning to feel sure of her end.

Most people liked Walter, even when they laughed at his simplicity, for it was the simplicity of a generous nature. We cannot therefore wonder if he was too confident, and from Lady Lufa's behavior presumed to think she looked upon him as worthy of a growing privilege. If she regarded literature as she professed to regard it, he had but to distinguish himself, he thought, to be more acceptable than wealth or nobility could have made him. As to material possibilities, the youth never thought of them. A worshiper does not meditate how to feed his goddess! Lady Lufa was his universe and everything in it—a small universe and scantily furnished for a human soul, even had she been the prime of women!

Walter scarcely thought of his home now, or of the father who made it home. As to God, it is hardly a question whether he had ever thought of him. For can that be called thinking of another which is the mere passing of a name (nay! the passing of a mere word) through the mind without one consequent thought of relation or duty—of how we stand before our Maker, and what responsibility of obedience we owe him? Many think it a horrible thing to say there is no God, who never think how much worse a thing it is not to heed him. If God be not worth obeying, what great ruin can it be to imagine his nonexistence?

What, then, had Walter made of it by leaving home? He had almost forgotten his father. He had learned to be at home in London. He had passed many judgments—some of them more or less just, all of them more or less unjust. He had printed enough for a volume of little better than truisms concerning life, society, fashion, dress, etc., and had published two or three rather nice poems. And now he had a small book of poetry almost ready. Finally, he had fallen in love with an earl's daughter.

"Everybody is gone," said Lady Lufa on the last day of the season. "And we are going tomorrow."

"Today," he rejoined, "London is full; tomorrow it will be a desert."

She looked up at him, and did not seem glad.

"I have enjoyed the season so much!" she said.

He thought her lip trembled.

"But you will come and see us in our country place at Combe-ridge, will you not?" she added.

"Do you think your mother will ask me?" he said.

"I think she will. I do so want to show you our library! And I have so many things to ask you!"

"I am your slave, the genie of your lamp."

"I would I had such a lamp as would call you!"

"It will need no lamp to make me come."

Lamps to attract moths are plentiful, and Lufa herself was one of the most brilliant.

11 / Where the Heart Is

London was very hot, very dusty, and as dreary as Walter had anticipated. When Lufa went, the moon went out of the heavens, the stars chose banishment with their mistress, and only the bright, labor-urging sun was left.

He might now take a holiday when he pleased, and he had money enough in hand to do so. His father wanted him to pay them a visit. But what if an invitation to Comberidge should arrive! And it would be so dull at home. He ought to go, he knew that. But he could not willingly run the risk of losing his delight, even for the sake of his first, best, and truest earthly friend.

But he must take his holiday now, in the slack of the London year, and the heat was great! He need not be all day with his father, and the thought of Lufa would be entrancing in the wide solitudes of the moor! Molly he scarcely thought of, and his aunt was to be forgotten. He would go for a few days, he said, thus keeping the door open for a speedy departure.

Just before he was about to leave, the invitation did arrive. With a sigh of relief he unpacked his bags. He would not have to endure the old place after all! But he had three or four days before he must leave. The next morning, to quiet the guilt that seemed insistent to rise from his conscience, he sat down at his writing table to compose a letter to his father. His heart warmed a little as he approached his home along the path of his memory, now somewhat more open to the better influences out of his past by his present sadness. Certain memories came to meet him. The thought of his mother was in the air. How long it was since she had spoken to him! He remembered her and his father watching by his bed while he tossed in a misery of which he could even now recall the prevailing delirious fancies. He remembered his mother's last rebuke to him—for insolence on his part to a servant; remembered her last embrace, her last words; and his heart turned tenderly to his father.

Yet when he attempted to put feelings to paper, he failed altogether, and an unexpected gloom overclouded him. Alas! he was not accustomed to write about his true self! Had he been heart-free and humble, penning words of tenderness would have been full of delight for him. But pride had been busy in his soul. Its home was in higher planes! What would Lady Lufa think of his homely *entourage,* his family—made up of a country farmer, an orphan, and a busybody aunt! Did such roots well become one of the second aristocracy? He had been gradually filling with a sense of importance—which had no being except in his own brain; and the notion took the meanest of mean forms—that of looking down on his own history.

No one needs find it hard to believe such snobbishness in a youth gifted like Walter Colman. For a sweet temper, fine sympathies, and warmth of affection cannot be called a man's own so long as he has felt and acted without co-operation of the will. And Walter had never yet fought a battle within himself. He had never set his will against his inclination. He had, indeed, bravely fronted the necessity of the world, but we cannot regard it as assurance of a noble nature that one is ready to labor for the things he needs. A man is contemptible indeed who is not ready to work. But not to be contemptible is hardly to be honorable. Walter had never actively *chosen* the right way, or put out any energy to walk in it. There are moneychangers and sinners nearer the kingdom of heaven than many a respectable, socially successful youth of education and ambition. Walter was not simple. He judged things not in themselves but after an artificial and altogether foolish standard, for his aim was a false one—social distinction.

The ways of his father's house were not in any way sordid or poor, though so simple that his financial losses had made scarcely a difference in them. They were hardly even humble—only old-fashioned. But as he imagined things now that his father was not a man of means, Walter found himself growing more and more ashamed of the soil whence he had sprung. He even found a minor incident now coming into his mind's eye, of Molly rising from the table to wait on her uncle or himself, bringing the teakettle in her own little brown hand, and he found himself mentally reproving her for such an unladylike action.

The notion that success lies in reaching the modes of life in the next higher social stratum, the fancy that those ways are the standard of what is worthy, becoming, or proper, the idea that our standing is determined by our knowledge of what is or is not *the accepted thing* is one of the degrading influences of modern times. It is only the lack of dignity at once and courtesy that makes such points of any interest or consequence.

As for Walter's thoughts about Molly, he could not bring himself to focus clearly upon her; either from indifference or preoccupation, he avoided any mental *tête-à-tête* with her with whom he had once shared as deeply as he had been capable. He had no true idea of the girl, neither indeed was capable of one. She was a whole nature; he was of many parts, not yet begun to cohere. This unlikeness probably was at the root of his thoughts, having avoided her since the day he left home. Perhaps he had an undefined sense of rebuke, and feared her without being aware of it. Never going further than halfway into a thing, he had never relished Molly's questions; they went deeper than he saw difficulty; he was not even conscious of the darkness upon which Molly desired light cast.

And now, as he became aware of her eyes looking at him through the unsettled regions of his conscience, he did not like it. Now that he thought about it, she had always been a bit pointed with him, as if she saw some lack of harmony between his consciousness and his history. He became annoyed, even irritated, with the memory of the olive-cheeked, black-eyed girl who had been for so many years like his sister. Even in her absence, she was making remarks upon him in that questioning laboratory of her brain!

After a few moments of attempting to address a few words to her, he dismissed the notion with a wave of the hand, quickly ended with a series of commonplaces to his father, signed his name, sealed the letter, and went out for a walk. It was some comfort at least, he said to himself as he went, that he was so soon to leave these uncongenial surroundings and go where all would be as a gentleman desired to see it, and where he would be appreciated for who he was!

The letter arrived at the farm. After the first initial greetings, in which some tenderness toward the old place and its people could be discerned, nothing came readily to follow. The wave had broken on the shore, and there was not another behind it. It was obvious to the father that the distance between them had widened. Yet when disappointed, he always tried to account for everything to the advantage of the other, and gave Walter every love-courtesy possible. He quite naturally showed the letter both to Miss Hancock and Molly.

Fortunately for Richard's even temper, his sister-in-law was discreetly silent, too busy sizing up the youth afresh to talk much; intent on material wherewith to make up her mind concerning him. She had to alter her idea of him as incapable of providing his own bread and cheese; but as to what reflection of him was henceforth to inhabit the glass of her judgment, she had not yet determined—further than that it should be an unfavorable one.

Molly, too, was quiet for a day or two. She had never felt Walter come very near her, for he was not one who had learned, or would easily learn, to give himself, and no man who does not give at least something of himself gives anything at all. But from his words to his father, she knew Walter had gone even further away. What would he say now when she offered him a penny for his thoughts? Would she even want to know them?

When Walter came home, he found bedtime a relief. He soon fell asleep, to dream of Lufa and the luxuries around her—things accumulated even to encumbrance, causing him to grow antagonistic to comfort, as Helots to liberty. How different from his dreams were the things of the humble farmhouse to the north!

How different his thoughts from those of the father who kneeled in the moonlight at the side of the bed and said something to him who never sleeps! When Walter woke, his first feeling was a pang: he was still in dreary London! Yet the days managed to pass, and on the third he found himself on his way to the train station, beside himself with anticipation.

12 / A Midnight Review

From Comberidge a cart had been sent to meet him at the railway. He drove up the avenue as the sun was setting behind the house, and its long, low, terraced front received him into a cold shadow.

The servant who opened the door said her ladyship was on the lawn. Following him across the hall, Walter came out into the glory of a red sunset. Like a lovely carpet, or rather like a green, silent river, the lawn appeared to flow from the house as from its fountain, issuing by the open doors and windows, and descending like a gentle rapid, to lose itself far away among trees and shrubs. Over it were scattered groups and couples and individuals, looking like the creatures of a half angelic paradise. A little way off, under the boughs of a huge beech tree, sat Lufa, reading with a pencil in her hand as if making notes.

As he stepped from the house, she looked up and saw him. She laid her book on the grass, rose, and came toward him. He went to meet her, but the light of the low sun was directly in his eyes, and he could not see her shadowed face. But her voice of welcome came out of the luminous darkness, and their hands found each other. He thought hers trembled, but it was his own. She led him to her mother.

"I am glad to see you," said Lady Tremaine. "You are just in time."

"For what, may I ask?" returned Walter.

"It is out at last!"

"No, Mamma," interrupted Lufa. "It is not out. The book is almost ready, but I have only one or two early copies. I am so glad Mr. Colman will be the first to see it! He will prepare me for the operation.''

"What do you mean?'' asked Walter, bewildered. It was the first word he had heard of her new book.

"Of course I shall be cut up! The weekly papers especially would lose half their readers did they not go in for literary vivisection! But Mamma shouldn't have asked you now.''

"Why?''

"Well—you might not—that is, I shouldn't like you to feel an atom less comfortable in speaking your mind about my verses.''

"There is no fear of that sort in my thoughts,'' answered Walter, laughing.

But it did trouble him a little that she had not let him know what she was doing.

"Besides,'' he went on, "you need never know what I think. There are other reviewers on the *Battery*!''

"I should recognize your hand anywhere! And more than that, I should only have to pick out the most rigid and unbending criticism to know which must be yours. It is your way, and you know it! Are you not always showing me up to myself! That's why I was in such mortal terror of your finding out what I was doing. If you had said anything to make me hate my work,'' she went on, looking up at him with earnest eyes, "I should never have touched it again, and I did so want to finish it! You have been my master now for—let me see—how many months . . .''

She paused, as if reflecting with pleasure, then quickly resumed. "I do not know how I shall ever thank you!'' Here she changed tone. "If I come off with a pound of flesh left, it will be owing entirely to the pains you have taken with me! I wonder whether you will like any of my triolets! But it is time to dress for dinner, so I will leave you in peace—but not all night, for when you go to bed you shall take *your* copy with you to help you fall asleep.''

While dressing, Walter was full of the dread of not liking the book well enough to praise it as he wished. A first book was nothing, he said to himself; it might be what it would. But a second—that was another matter! He recalled what first books he knew. Both Shelley's and Byron's were so bad as to be below criticism. He knew what followed theirs, but what had followed Lady Lufa's? What if it should be no better than what preceded!

For his own part, he would not much care. It was not for her poetry; it was for herself he loved her! What she wrote could make no difference. Of course it was good that she had some genuine understanding of poetry, and admiration and feeling for it. A poet could do well enough with a wife who never wrote a verse, but hardly with one who had no natural relation to it, no perception what it was. A poet in love with one who laughed at poetry! What could possibly be their relation to each other? He is a poor poet—and Walter was such a poet—who does not know there are better things than poetry.

Walter feared the coming gift as he might that of a doubted enchantress. It was not the less a delight, however, to remember that she said "your copy." But he must stop thinking and put on his necktie! There are other things than time and tide that wait for no man!

Lady Tremaine gave him Lufa, and she took his arm with old familiarity. The talk at the table was but such as it could hardly help being—for Walter it only mattered that Lufa was in the middle of it! The pleasure of talk often owes not much to the sense of it. There is more than the intellect concerned in talk; there is more at its root than fact or logic, words or ideas.

When the scene changed to the drawing room, Lufa played tolerably and sang well, delighting Walter. She asked and received his permission to sing "my song," as she called it, and pleased him with it more than ever. He managed to get her into the conservatory, which was large, and there he talked much, and she seemed to listen. It was but the vague, twilit, allusive talk which, coming readily to all men in love, came the more readily to one always a poet, and not merely a poet by being in love. Everyone in love sees a little further into things, but few see clearly, and hence love talk has in general so little meaning. Ordinary men in love gain glimpses of truth beyond what they are usually able to see, but from having so little dealing with the truth, poets do not even try to get a hold of it. They do not know it for truth even when dallying with it. It is the true man's dreams that come true.

He raised her hand to his lips as at length she turned back toward the drawing room, and he thought she more than yielded, but could not be sure. Anyhow she was not offended, for she smiled with her usual sweetness as she bade him good night.

"One moment, Mr. Colman!" she added. "I promised you a sedative! I will run and get it.—No, I won't keep you. I will send it to your room."

They parted. It was late, and he went to his room in the ecstasy of exhaustion. He had scarcely shut the door when it opened again. There was Lufa.

"I beg your pardon," she said. "I thought you would not yet be here, and I wanted to make my little offering with my own hand: it owes so much to you!"

She slipped past him, laid her book on his table, and went.

He lighted his candles with eager anxiety, then picked up the volume. It was a dramatic poem of some length, daintily bound in white vellum with gilt edges. On the title page was written "The Master's copy," with the date and Lufa's initials. He threw himself into a great soft chair that with open arms invited him, and began to read.

He had taken champagne pretty freely at dinner. His mind was yet in the commotion left by the summer wind of their many words that might mean so much. He felt his kiss of her dainty hand, and her pressure of it to his lips. As he read, she seemed still and always in the doorway, entering with the book. Its inscription was continually turning up with a shine. Such was the mood in which he read the poem.

Through it he read, every word, some of it many times. Then he rose and went to his writing table to set down his judgment of the lady's poem.

He wrote and wrote, almost without a pause. The dawn began to glimmer, the red blood of the morning came back to chase the swoon of the night before at last, throwing down his pen, he gave a sigh of weary joy, tore off his clothes, and plunged into his bed, and there lay afloat on the soft waves of sleep.

And as he slept, the sun came slowly up to shake the falsehood out of the earth.

13 / Reflection

Walter slept until nearly noon, then rose, very weary, but with a gladness at his heart. On his table were spread such pages as must please Lufa!

His thoughts went back to the poem, but to his uneasy surprise, he found he did not recall it with any special pleasure. He had great delight in reading it and in giving shape to his delight, but he could not now think what kind of thing it was that had given him such satisfaction.

He had worked too long, he said to himself, and this was the reaction: he was too tired to enjoy the memory of what he had so heartily admired. Aesthetic judgment was so dependent on mood! He would glance over what he had done, correct it a little, and enclose it in the afternoon's mail that it might appear in the next issue of the journal.

He drank the cup of cold tea by his bedside, sat down, and took up his hurriedly written sheets. He found in them much that seemed good work of his own, and the passages quoted gave ostensible ground for the remarks made upon them. But somehow the whole affair seemed quite different. The review would make any lover of verse want to read the book, and the passages cited were preceded and followed by rich and praiseful epithets. But neither quotations nor remarks moved in him any echo of response. He gave the manuscript what correction it required, which was not much, for Walter was an accurate as well as ready writer, then laid it aside and took up the poem.

What could be the matter? There was nothing but dying embers where last night had been glow and flame! Something must be amiss with him!

He recalled an occasion on which, feeling similarly cold toward certain poems that had till then been favorites, he was sorely troubled. But a serious attack of illness soon relieved his perplexity: something like that must surely be at hand for him not to account for the contradiction between Walter last night and Walter this morning. He must be getting sick!

Closer and closer he scanned what he read, peering as if he might see to its very roots, agonizing to see what he had seen as he wrote. But his critical consciousness would not acknowledge what he had felt. He read on and on, read the poem through, turned back, read passage after passage again, but without one individual approach to the revival of the former impression. "Commonplace! Commonplace!" echoed in his inner ear as if whispered by some mocking spirit. He argued that he had often found himself too particular. His demand for polish ruined many of his verses, rubbing and melting and wearing them away, like frost and wind and rain, till they were worthless! The predominance and overkeenness of the critical had turned to disease in him! His eye was sharpened to see the point of a needle, but not the shape of a tree.

A man's mind was meant to receive as a mirror, not to concentrate rays like a convex lens! Was it not then likely that the first reading gave the true impression of the ethereal, the vital, the flowing, the iridescent? Did not the solitary and silent night brood like a hen on the nest of the poet's imaginings? Was it not the night that waked the soul? How then could the light of the garish day afford the mood fit for judging a poem—the cold sick morning, when life is but half worth living!

Walter did not stop to think how much champagne he had taken, nor how much that fact might have to do with his altered judgment. For it would have been horrible to him to think that the morning was the clear-eyed, and that the praise he had lavished on the book was but a vapor of the night. How was he to carry himself to the lady of his love, who at most did not care half as much for him as for her book?

How poetry could be such a passion with her when her own

was but mediocre was a question Walter dared not shape—not, however, because he saw the same question might be put with regard to himself: his own poetry was neither strong nor fresh nor revealing. He had not noted that an unpoetic person will occasionally go into a mild ecstasy over phrase or passage or verse in which a poet may see little or nothing.

Finally he came to this conclusion—his one hour had as good a claim to insight as his other. If he had seen the thing so once, why not say what he had seen? Why should not the review stand? His consciousness of the night before had certainly been nearer that of a complete, capable being than that of today! He had been in a higher human condition then than now!

But then a new doubt assailed him: what was he to conclude concerning his other numerous reviews? Was he influencing the world's opinion of the labor of hundreds of writers merely according to the mood he happened to be in, or at the hour at which he read their volumes? And if he had to scrap his first and write *another* judgment of that poem in vellum and gold, he must first pack his bag! To write in her home as he now felt would be treachery!

Not confessing it to his mind, he was gradually persuading himself to send the review as it was. Of course, were he writing it now, he could not write a paper such as lay before him! But the thing being written, it could claim as good a chance of being right as another. Had it not been written as honestly as another of today would be? Might it not be just as true? The laws of art were so undefined!

Thus on and on went the windmill of heart and brain until at last the devil, or the devil's shadow—that is, the bad part of the man himself—got the better of him; and Walter, not being for the truth, did what was untrue—published the thing he would no longer have said. He thought he worshiped the truth, but he did not. He knew that the truth was everything, but the lie that came seemed better than the truth. In his soul he knew he was not acting truly; that had he honestly loved the truth, he would not have played such hocus-pocus with metaphysics and logic, but would have hastily walked toward a manly conclusion in the matter. But he was not yet a man. Thus, he took the packet, and on his way to the dining room, dropped it into the postbox in the hall.

During lunch he was rather silent and abstracted: the packet was not gone, and his conscience might yet command him to recall it! When the hour was past, and the paper beyond recovery, he felt easier, saying to himself, what was done was done and could not be undone; he would be more careful another time. One comfort was that at least he had done no injustice to Lufa. He did not reflect that he had done her the greatest injustice of all in helping her to believe that worthy which was not worthy, herself worshipful who was not worshipful. He told her that he finished her drama before going to bed, and was perfectly charmed with it. That it as much exceeded his expectations then as it had fallen below them since, he did not say.

In the evening he was not so bright as before. Lufa saw it and was troubled. She feared he doubted the success of her poem. She opened the discussion and led the way, and found he avoided talking about it. She began to fear he was not so well pleased with it as he had said. Walter asked if he might not read it from the drawing room. She would not consent.

"There are none here of our sort," she said. "They think literature foolish. Even my mother, the best of mothers, doesn't care about poetry, cannot tell one measure from another. Come and read a page or two of it in the summer house, just the two of us in the wilderness instead. I want to know how it will sound in people's ears."

Walter was ready enough. He was fond of reading aloud, and believed he could so read the poem that he need not comment upon it. And certainly, if justice meant making words express more than was in them, he did it justice. But in truth the situation within the poetic drama was sometimes touching, and all the more so to Walter that the hero of the slender story was the lady's inferior birth, means, and position—much more her inferior than Walter was Lufa's. The lady alone was on the side of the lowly born; father, mother, brothers, sisters, uncles, aunts, and cousins were all against him even to hatred. The general pathos of the idea disabled the criticism of the audience, composed of the authoress and the reader, blinding perhaps both to not a little that was neither brilliant nor poetic.

The lady wept at the sound of her own verses from the lips of one who was to her in the position of the hero toward the heroine, and the lover—critic as he was—could not but be touched when he saw her weep at passages suggesting his relation to her, so that, when they found the hand of the one resting in that of the other, it did not seem strange to either. When suddenly the lady snatched hers away, it was only because a mischievous little bird spying them, and hurrying away to tell, made a great fluttering in the foliage. Then was Walter's conscience not a little consoled, for he was aware of a hearty love for the poem.

Under such conditions he could have gone on reading it all the night!

14 / A Ride Together _____

Days passed and things went on much the same, Walter not daring to tell the girl all he felt, but seizing every opportunity of a *tête-à-tête*, and missing none of the proximity she allowed him, and she never seeming other than pleased to be his companion. Her ways with him were always pretty, and sometimes playful. She was almost studious to please him, and if she never took a liberty with him, she never resented any he took with her, which certainly were neither numerous nor daring, for Walter was not presumptuous, least of all with women.

But Lufa was careful not to neglect their other guests. She was always ready to accompany any of the ladies riding in the morning, and a Mr. Sefton, who was there when Walter arrived, generally rode with them. He was older than Walter, and had taken little notice of him, which Walter resented more than he would have cared to acknowledge. He was tall and lanky, with a look of not having been in the oven quite long enough, but handsome nevertheless. Without an atom of contempt, he cared nothing for what people might think, and when accused of anything, laughed, and never defended himself. Having no doubt he was in the right, he had no anxiety as to the impression he might make. In the hunting field he was now reckless, now so cautious that the men would kid him. But they knew well enough that whatever he did came either of pure whim or downright good sense; no one ever questioned his pluck. I believe an intermittent laziness had something to do with his inconsistency.

It had been taken for granted by Lufa that Walter knew nothing of horses and could not ride, whereas, not only had he had some experience, but he was of the few possessed of an individual influence over the lower brotherhood of animals, and his was especially equine.

One morning, from an ailment in one of the horses, Lufa found that her mount required consideration. Sefton said the horse he had been riding would carry her perfectly.

"What will *you* do for a horse?" she asked.

"Go without," answered Sefton.

"What shall we ladies do for a gentleman to accompany us?"

"Go without. I'm sure you shall manage."

"I saw a groom this morning, on a lovely little roan," suggested Walter, who was standing by as the riding party made ready to depart.

"Ah, Red Racket!" answered Lady Lufa. "He is no horse. He is a little fiend. Goes as gently as a lamb with my father, though, or anyone that he knows can ride him. Try Red Racket, George," she added to Sefton. They were cousins, though not in the next degree.

"I would if I could stay on him. But I'm not a rough rider, and much disinclined to have my bones broken. No, thank you!"

"Come, George," said his sister, "you will make them think you are no horseman!"

"Which is precisely the truth! I do not have a good seat, and I am not going to make a fool of myself by being urged. I know what I can and can't do."

"I wish I had the chance," said Walter, as if to himself, but so that Lufa heard.

"You can ride?" said Lufa with pleased surprise.

"Why not?" returned Walter. "Every Englishman should ride."

"Yes. And every Englishman should swim, but Englishmen are drowned every day."

"That is as often because they can swim, but do not have Mr. Sefton's prudence."

"You mustn't think my cousin afraid of Red Racket!" she returned.

"I don't. He doesn't look like it."

"Do you really wish to ride the roan?"

"Indeed I do!"

"I will order him round," she said, rising.

Walter did not quite enjoy her consenting so easily: had she no fear for him of the risk Mr. Sefton would not run?

"She wants me to cut a good figure!" he said to himself, and went to get ready.

I have no particular deed of prowess on Walter's part to record. There was need for none. The instant he was in the saddle, Red Racket recognized a master.

"You can't have ridden him before?" questioned Lufa.

"I never saw him till this morning."

"He likes you, I suppose," she said.

As they returned across the fields an hour later, the other ladies being in front, and the groom some distance behind, Walter brought his roan side by side with Lufa's horse.

"You know Browning's *Last Ride Together*?" he asked.

"Yes," she answered, with a faint blush; "but this is not our last ride! It is our first! Why didn't you tell me you were such a horseman? We might have had many rides together."

"Promise me a last one," he said.

"How can I? How should I know it was the last?"

"Promise," he persisted, "that if ever you see just one last ride possible, you will let me know."

She hesitated a moment, then answered.

"I will."

"Thank you!" said Walter with fervor.

As by consent, they rode after the others.

Walter had not yet summoned his courage to say anything definite. But he had said many things that must have compelled her to imagine what he had not said. Therefore the promise she had given him seemed encouraging. They rode in silence the rest of the way back to the house.

It was the last ride for the present because of a change in the weather. In a few days came the next issue of the *Field Battery* with Walter's review, bringing a revival of the self-reproach he had begun to forget. The paper felt in his hand like bad news or something nasty. He could not bear the thought of having to take his part in the talk it would undoubtedly occasion. It could not now be helped, however, and that was a great comfort! It was impossible, nonetheless, to keep it up. As he had foreseen, all this time came no revival of his first impression of the poem. He went to find his hostess, and told her he must go to London that same afternoon.

As he took his leave, he put the paper in Lufa's hand, saying, "You will find there what I have said about the poem."

15 / Walter's Book

I need hardly say he found his first lonely evening back in his London lodgings dull. He was not yet capable of looking beneath the look of anything. He felt cabined, cribbed, confined. His world-clothing came too near him. From the flowing robes of a park, a great house, large rooms, wide staircases—with plenty of air and space, color, softness, fitness, completeness—he found himself in the worn, tight, shabby garment of his cheap London room!

But Walter, far from being a wise man, was not therefore a fool. He was not one whom this world cannot teach, and who has therefore to be sent to some idiot asylum in the next before sense can be got into him, or, rather, out of him. No man is a fool who having work to do sets himself to do it, and this Walter did.

He had begun a poem as the opening entry for a volume, of which the rest was nearly ready. Into this lengthy opening piece, he now set himself to weave a sequel to her drama, from the point where she had left the story. Every hour he could spare from drudgery he devoted to it—urged by the delightful prospect of letting Lufa see what he could do. Gaining facility with his stanza as he went on, the pleasure of it grew, and more than comforted his loneliness. Sullivan could hardly ever get him out of his room.

Finding a young publisher prepared to undertake half the risk, on the ground, unexpressed, of the author's proximity to the judgment seat, Walter was ecstatic. Too experienced to hope for any profit, he yet hoped to clear his expenses, and therefore borrowed heavily for his half of the capital required. Walter thus became liable for much more than he possessed.

He had one little note from Lufa, concerning a point in rhythm which perplexed her. She had a good ear, and was conscientious in her mechanics. But she understood nothing of the broken music which a master of verse will turn to such high service. There are lines in Milton that Walter, who knew far more than she, could not read until long after, when Dante taught him how.

In the month of December came another note from Lady Lufa, inviting him to spend a week with them after Christmas.

"Perhaps then we may have yet a ride together," added a postscript.

"What does she mean?" thought Walter, a pale fear at his heart. "She cannot mean our last ride!"

One conclusion he came to—that he must tell her plainly he loved her. The thing was only right, though of course ridiculous in the eyes of worldly people, said the far from unworldly poet. True, she was the daughter of an earl, and he the son of a farmer, and those who called the land their own looked down upon those who tilled it. But a banker, or a brewer, or the son of a contractor who had wielded the spade might marry an earl's daughter. Why should not the son of a farmer—not to say one who, according to the lady's mother, himself belonged to an aristocracy? The farmer's son indeed was poor, and who would look at a poor banker or a poor brewer more than a poor farmer! It was all money! But was he going to give in to that? Was he to grant that possession made a man honorable, and the lack of it despicable! To act as if she could think in such a silly fashion would be to insult her! He would lay bare his heart. There were things in it which she knew what value to set upon—things as far ahead of birth as birth was ahead of money! He would accept the invitation, and if possible get his volume out before the day mentioned, so as, he hoped, to be a little in the mouth of the public when he went!

Walter, like many another youth, imagined the way to make a woman love him was to humble himself before her, tell her how beautiful she was, and how much he loved her. I do not see why any woman should therefore love a man. If she loves him already, anything will do to make her love him more; if she does not, no entreaty will wake what is not there to be waked. Every wrong and cruelty and carelessness may increase love already rooted; but neither love, nor kindness, nor worship will prevail to plant it.

In his formal acceptance of the invitation, he enclosed some verses destined for his volume, in which he poured out his boyish passion over his lady's hair, and eyes, and hands—a poem not without some of the merits made much of by the rising school of the day, and possessing qualities higher, perhaps, than those upon which that school chiefly prided itself. She made, as he expected, no acknowledgment, but neither did she return the verses.

Lyric after lyric, with Lufa for its inspiration, he wrought, like damask flowers, into his poem. Every evening, and all the evening, sometimes late into the morning, he fashioned and filed until at length it was finished and sent to the publisher.

When some weeks later, the toiling girl who waited on him appeared with the proof-sheets in her hand for his final inspection, she came like a winged ministrant laying a wondrous gift before him. And in truth, poor as he came to think it, was it not a gift greater than any angel could have brought him? Was not the seed of his own poetry sown in his being by him that loved him before he was? These verses were the poor first flowers come to make way for better—themselves a gift none but God could give.

The book was now rapidly approaching its birth, as the day of Lufa's summons drew near. He had inscribed the volume to her, not by name, but in a dedication she could not but understand and no other possibly could, founded on her promise of a last ride: it was so delightful to have a secret with her! He hoped to the last to be able to take a copy with him, but was disappointed by some contretemps connected with the binding—about which he was as particular as if it had been itself a poem. Thus he had to pack his bag empty-handed, and leave his book behind him in London.

Almost continuously on his way to the station, he kept repeating to himself: "Is it to be the last ride, or only another?"

16 / A Winter Afternoon's Story

When Walter arrived he found the paradise under snow. But the summer had only run indoors, and there was blooming. Lufa was kinder than ever, but, he fancied, a little embarrassed, which he interpreted to his advantage. He was shown into the room he had occupied before.

It did not take him long to learn the winter ways of the house. Mr. and Miss Sefton were there, and all seemed glad of his help to ward off consciousness, for there could be no riding so long as the frost lasted and the snow kept falling, and the ladies did not care to go out. And in some country houses Time has as many lives as a cat, and needs a great deal of killing—a butchery to be one day bitterly repented, perhaps. But as a savage cannot be a citizen, so cannot people of fashion belong to the kingdom of heaven. Anyhow, Sefton managed to still several of the old cat's lives with his stories.

The third morning brought a thaw, with a storm of wind and rain, and after lunch they gathered in the gloomy library and began to tell ghost stories. Walter happened to know a few of the rarer sort, and found himself in his element. His art came to help him, as well as the eyes of the ladies, and he rose to his best. As he was working one of his tales to its climax, Mr. Sefton entered the room, where Walter had been the only gentleman, and took a chair beside Lufa.

She rose, saying, "I beg your pardon, Mr. Colman, but would you mind stopping a minute while I get a little more red silk for my imperial dragon? Mr. Sefton has already taken the sting out of the snake!"

"What snake?" asked Sefton.

"The snake of terror," she answered. "Did you not see him as you came in—erect on his coiled tail, drawing his head back for a darting spring? Until you made him disappear with your entrance."

"I am very sorry," said Sefton. "I hope everybody will pardon my rudeness."

When Lufa had found her silk, she took a seat nearer to Walter, who resumed and finished his narrative.

"I wonder she lived to tell about it!" said one of the ladies.

"I do not see why," rejoined their hostess, "everyone should be so terrified at the thought of meeting a ghost! It seems to me cowardly."

"I don't think it cowardly," said Sefton, "to be frightened at a ghost, or at anything else."

"Now don't say you would run away!" remonstrated his sister.

"I couldn't very well, don't you know, if I was in bed! But I might—I don't know—hide my head under the blankets!"

"I don't believe it a bit!"

"To be sure," continued Sefton reflectively, "there does seem a difference. To hide is one thing, and to run is another—quite another thing! If you are frightened, you are frightened and you can't help it. But if you run away, then you are a coward. Yes, quite true! And yet there are some things men, whom other men would be afraid to call cowards, would run from fast enough!—Your story, Mr. Colman," he went on, "reminds me of an adventure I had—if that be an adventure where there was no danger—except, indeed, of losing my wits, which Lufa would say was no great loss. I don't often tell the story, for I have an odd weakness for being believed, and nobody ever does believe that story, though it is as true as I live. And when a thing is true, the blame lies with those that don't believe it. Aren't you of my mind, Mr. Colman?"

"You had better not appeal to him!" said Lufa. "Mr. Colman does not believe a word of the stories he has been telling. He regards them entirely from the artistic point of view, and cares only for their effect. He is writing a novel and wants to study people under a ghost story."

"I don't altogether endorse your judgment of me, Lady Lufa," said Walter, who did not quite like what she said. "I am ready to believe anything in which I can see reason. I should like very much to hear Mr. Sefton's story. I never saw the man that saw a ghost, unless Mr. Sefton is that man."

"You shall say what you will when you have heard," replied Sefton. "I shall offer no explanation, only tell you what I saw, or, if you prefer, what I experienced. You must then fall back on your own views of metaphysics and spiritual matters for an explanation. I don't myself care what anybody thinks about it."

"You are not very polite!" said Lufa.

"Only truthful," replied Sefton.

"Please go on."

"We are dying to hear."

Sefton shuffled himself in his chair and was silent a few moments, as if arranging his thoughts.

"Well, here goes!" he began. "I was staying at a country house—"

"Not here, I hope!" interrupted Lufa.

"I have reasons for not saying where it was, or where it wasn't. It may have been in Ireland, it may have been in Scotland, it may have been in England. It was in one of the three, I will say that much—in an old house, parts of it *very* old."

He paused momentarily, took a breath, then continued.

"One morning I happened to be late, and found the breakfast table deserted. I was not the last to come down, however, for presently another man appeared, whom I had met at dinner the day before for the first time. We both happened to be in the army, and had drawn a little together in our conversation. The moment I saw him, I knew he had passed an uncomfortable night. His face was like dough, with livid spots under the eyes. He sat down and poured himself out a cup of tea.

" 'Game pie?' I said, but he did not heed me.

"There was nobody in the room but the two of us, and I thought it best to leave him alone. 'Are you an old friend of the family?' he asked at length. 'About the age of most friends,' I answered. He was silent again for a bit, then said, 'I'm going to leave!'

"I remained silent, thinking his statement must have something to do with a certain lady in the house with us.

" 'No, it's not that!' he said, reading my thought exactly.

" 'It's not that I want to know why,' I replied.

" 'Neither do I want to tell,' he rejoined. 'But what I do want is for you to tell Mrs.—'

"There! I was on the very verge of saying her name! And you would have known who she was, all of you! I am glad I caught myself in time!

" '—tell Mrs. Blank,' he said, 'why I went.'

" 'Very well, I will,' I said. 'Why *are* you going?'

" 'Can't you help a fellow by making up an excuse? I'm not going to give *her* the reason.'

" 'Tell me what you want me to say, and I will tell her you told me to say so.'

" 'Oh, all right! I will tell *you* the truth.'

" 'Fire away, then,' I said.

" 'I was beastly afraid last night,' he said. 'I daresay you think as I did that a man ought never to be a hair off the cool.'

" 'That depends,' I replied. 'There are some things, and there may be more, at which any but an idiot might well be scared. But some fools are such fools they can't shiver! What's the matter? I'll give you my word I'll not make game of it.'

"The fellow looked so seedy, don't you know, I couldn't but be brotherly, or at least cousinly to him—though that doesn't go for much, does it, Lufa?

" 'Well,' the fellow said, 'I will tell you. Last night I had been in bed about five minutes, and hadn't even had time to grow sleepy, when I heard a curious shuffling in the passage outside my door, and an indescribable terror came over me. To be perfectly open with you, however, I had heard that was the sign she was coming!'

" 'Who was coming?' I asked.

" 'The ghost, of course!' he answered.

" 'The ghost!'

" 'You don't mean to say you never heard of the ghost?'

" 'Never heard a word of it.'

" 'Well, they don't like to speak of it, but everybody knows it!'

" 'Go on,' I said, and he did, but plainly with a tearing effort.

" 'The shuffling was like feet in slippers much too big. As if I had been five instead of thirty-five, I dived under the blankets, and lay so for minutes after the shuffling had ceased. But at length I persuaded myself it was but a foolish fancy and I had never really heard anything. What with fear and heat I was greatly out of breath too, I can tell you! So I came to the surface and looked out from my blanket covering.'

"Here he paused a moment and looked almost livid.

" 'There stood a horrible old woman, staring at me as if she had been seeing me all the time, and as if the blankets made no difference!'

" 'Was she really ugly?' I asked.

" 'Well, I don't know what you call ugly,' he answered, 'but if you had seen her stare, you would have thought her ugly enough! Had she been beautiful, though, I don't imagine I should have been less frightened!'

" 'Well,' I said, for he had come to a pause, 'and what came next?'

" 'I cannot tell. I came to myself all trembling, and as cold and as wet as if I had been swimming in a well.'

" 'You are sure you were not dreaming?' I asked.

" 'I was not, but I do not expect you to believe me!'

" 'You must not be offended,' I said, 'if I find the thing stiff to stow! I believe you all the same.'

" 'What?' he said, not quite understanding me.

" 'An honest man and a gentleman,' I answered.

" 'And a coward to boot!'

" 'God forbid!' I returned. 'What man can answer for himself at every moment. If I remember, Hector turned at last and ran from Achilles!'

"He said nothing, and I went on. 'I once heard a preaching fellow say, "When a wise man is always wise, then is the kingdom of heaven!" and I thought he knew something!' I talked, don't you know, to quiet him. 'I once saw,' I said, 'the best-tempered man I ever knew, in the worst rage I ever saw man in—though I must allow he had good reason!' He drank his cup of tea, got up, and said, 'I'm off. Goodbye—and thank you! A million pounds wouldn't make me stay in this house another hour! There is that in it I fear ten times worse than the ghost.'

" 'Gracious! what is that?' I said.

" 'This horrible cowardice oozing from her like a mist. The house is full of it! It came over me last night!'

" 'But what shall I say to Mrs. Blank?'

" 'Anything you like.'

" 'I will say then, that you are very sorry, but were compelled to go.'

" 'Say what you please, only let me go! Tell them to send my traps along after me. Goodbye. I'm in a sepulchre! I shall have to give up my commission if I cannot shake this miserable cowardice!' And so he went."

"And what became of him?"

"I've neither seen nor heard of him to this day."

He ceased with the cadence of an ended story.

"Is that all?"

"You spoke of an adventure of your own!"

"I was hoping," said Lufa, "that in our house Mr. Colman was at last to hear a ghost story from the man's own lips."

"The sun is coming out!" said Sefton, glancing around and paying no heed to everyone's objections. "I think I shall walk out to the stables and enjoy a cigar."

The company protested, but he turned a deaf ear to expostulation, and went.

17 / A Winter Evening's Story

In the drawing room after dinner, some of the ladies gathered about him, and begged Sefton to tell the story of his own adventure. He smiled queerly.

"Very well, you shall have it!" he answered.

They seated themselves, and the company came from all parts of the room—among the rest, Lufa and Walter.

"It was three days, if I remember," began Sefton, "after my military friend left, when one night I found myself alone in the drawing room, just waked from a little doze. No one had said good night to me. I looked at my watch; it was half past eleven. I rose and went. My bedroom was up on the first floor.

"The stairs were peculiar—a construction later than much of the house, but by no means modern. When you reached the landing of the first floor and looked up, you could see above you the second floor, defended by a balustrade between the arches. There were no carpets on stairs or landings, which were all of oak.

"I cannot say what made me look up. But I think, indeed I am almost sure, I had heard a noise like that the ghost was said to make, as of one walking in shoes too large; and when I did look I saw a lady looking down over the balusters on the second floor. I thought someone was playing me a trick, and imitating the ghost, for the ladies had been chaffing me a good deal that night; they often do. She wore an old-fashioned, brown, silky looking dress. I rushed up to see who was taking the rise out of me. I looked up at her as I ran, and she kept looking down, but apparently not at me. Her face was that of a middle-aged woman, beginning, indeed, to be old, and had an intent, rather troubled

101

look, I should say, but I did not consider that closely.

"I was at the top in a moment, on the level where she stood leaning over the handrail. I turned and approached her. Apparently she neither saw nor heard me. 'Well done!' I said to myself; 'what a splendid acting job!' But even then I was beginning to be afraid, without knowing why. Every man's impulse, I fancy, is to go right up to anything that frightens him—at least, I have always found it so. I walked close up to the woman. She moved her head and turned in my direction, but only as if about to go away. Whether she looked at me I cannot tell, but I saw her eyes plain enough. By this time, I suppose, the idea of a ghost must have been uppermost to me, for, being now quite close to her, I put out my hand as if to touch her. *My hand went through her— through her head and body!* I am not joking in the least. I mean you to believe, if you can, exactly what I say. What she then did, or whether she took any notice of my movement, I cannot tell, I only know what I did, or rather what I did not do. For had I been capable of it, I should have cried out in a shriek that would have filled the house with ghastliest terror. But there was a load of iron on my chest, and the hand of a giant at my throat. I could not help opening my mouth, for something drew all the muscles of my jaw and throat, but I could not utter a sound. The horror I was in was entirely new to me, and no more under my control than a fever. I only wonder it did not paralyze me, for I was able to turn and run down the stairs. I ran as if all the sins of my life were at my heels! I flew, never seeming to touch the stairs as I went. I darted along the passage, burst into my room, shut and locked the door, lighted all the candles I could lay my hands on, fell into a chair, shuddered, and gradually began to breathe again."

He ceased, not without present signs of the agitation he described. "But that's not all!"

"What else happened . . . tell us more."

"I have nothing more to tell," answered Sefton. "But I haven't stopped wondering what could have frightened me so. You can't imagine what it was like!"

"I know I should have been worse," said one of the ladies.

"Perhaps—but why? Why should anyone have been terrified? The poor thing had lost her body, it is true; but there she was notwithstanding—all the same! It might be nicer or not so nice to her, but why should it so affect me, that's what I want to know. I don't see the sense of it! I am sure that one meets constantly— sits down with, eats and drinks with, hears sing and play, and remark on the weather or the fate of the nation . . ."

He paused, his eyes fixed on Walter.

"What are you driving at?" said Lufa.

"I was thinking of a much more fearful kind of creature," he answered.

"What kind of creature?" she asked.

"A creature," he said slowly, "that *has* a body but no soul to go with it. All body, with brain enough to manage its affairs, yet it has *no* soul. Such will never wander about after they are dead! There will be nothing to wander! Good night, ladies! Were I to tell you the history of a woman whose acquaintance I made some years ago at Baden, you would understand the sort. Good night!"

There was silence for a moment or two. Had his sister not been present, something other than complimentary to Sefton might have crept about the drawing room—to judge from the expression on two or three faces. Walter felt the man worth knowing, but felt also something about him that repelled him.

18 / The Soulless

In his room Walter threw himself in a chair and sat without thinking, for the mental presence of Lufa was hardly thought.

Gradually Sefton's story revived, and for a time displaced the image of Lufa. It was the only firsthand authenticated ghost narration he had ever heard. His imagination alone had till then been attracted by such tales. But this brought him close to things of import as profound as marvelous. He began to wonder how he was likely to carry himself in such an interview. Courage such as Mr. Sefton's he dared not claim—any more than hope for the distinction of ever putting his hand through a ghost! To be sure, the question philosophically considered, Sefton could have done no such thing. For where no relation existed, he reasoned, or rather assumed, the one could not be materially present to the other. *A fortiori*—there could be no passing of the one through the other! Where the ghost was, the hand was; both existed in the same space at the same time; therefore the one did not penetrate the other. The ghost, he held, never saw Sefton, knew or thought of his presence, or was aware of any intrusive outrage from his hand! He shrank, nonetheless, however, from such phantasmic presence as Sefton had described. A man's philosophy made but a fool of him when it came to the pinch! He would indeed like to see a ghost, but not to be alone with one!

Here came back to him a certain look in Lufa's face, which he had not understood: was it possible she knew something about the thing? Could this be the house where it took place, where the ghost appeared? The room in which he sat was very old! The pictures in it none but for their age would hang upon any wall.

And the bed was huger and gloomier than he had ever seen elsewhere! It was on the second floor too! What if this was the very room the officer slept in!

He must run into port, find shelter from the terrors of the shoreless sea of the unknown. But the only harbor he could seek was the bed and closed eyes!

The dark is a strange refuge from the darkness—yet that which most men seek. It is so dark—let us go further from the light! Thus deeper they go, and come upon greater terrors! He undressed hurriedly, blew out his candles, and by the light of the fire, glowing rather than blazing, plunged into the expanse that glimmered before him like a lake of sleep in the moonshine of dreams.

The moment he laid down his head, he became aware of what seemed an unnatural stillness. Throughout the evening a strong wind had been blowing about the house. It had now ceased, and without having noted the storm, Walter was now aware of the calm.

But what made him so cold? The surface of the linen was like a film of ice! He rolled himself round, and like a hedgehog, he sought shelter within the circumference of his own person. But he could not get warm, lie as close as he might to his own door; there was no admittance! Had the room suddenly turned cold? Could it be that the ghost was near, making the air like that of the grave from which she had come out? For such ghosts as walk the world at night, what refuge so fit as their tombs in the daytime! The thought was a worse horror than he had known himself capable of feeling. He shivered with the cold. It seemed to pierce to his very bones. A strange and hideous constriction seized the muscles of his neck and throat: had not Sefton described the sensation? Was it not a sure sign of ghostly presence?

How much longer he could have endured, or what would have been the result of the prolongation of his suffering, I cannot tell. Molly would have found immediate refuge with him to whom belong all the ghosts wherever they roam or rest—with him who can deliver from the terrors of the night as well as from the perplexities of the day. But Walter felt his lonely being exposed on all sides.

The handle of the door moved. I am not sure whether ghosts always enter and leave a room in silence, but the sound horribly shook Walter's nerves, and nearly made an end of him for a time. But a voice said, "May I come in?"

What he answered or whether he answered, Walter could not have told, but his terror subsided. The door opened wider, someone entered, closed it softly, and approached the bed through the dull firelight.

"I did not think you would be in bed!" said the voice, which Walter now knew for Sefton's, "but at the risk of waking you, even of giving you a sleepless night, I must have a little talk with you."

"I shall be glad for it," answered Walter, desperately trying to hide the trembling of his knees. Sefton little realized how welcome indeed was his visit!

But he was come to do him a service for which he could hardly at once be grateful. The *best* things done for any are generally those for which they are at the moment *least* grateful; it needs the result of the service to make them able to prize it.

Walter thought perhaps he had more of the story to tell—something he had not chosen to talk of to the ladies.

Sefton stood, and for a few minutes there was silence. He seemed to be meditating, yet looked like one who wanted to light his cigar.

"Won't you take a seat?" said Walter.

"Thank you," returned Sefton, and sat on the bed.

"I am twenty-seven," he said at length. "How old are you?"

"Twenty-three," answered Walter.

"When I was twenty-three, I knew so much more than I do now. So I thought at least. I'm not half so sure about things as I was then. I wonder if you will find it so."

"I hope so—otherwise I won't have made much progress."

"Well now, couldn't you just—why not?—quicken your progress by making use of my experience?"

"I don't quite follow you."

"I'm talking like a fool, I know, but never mind; what I'm

trying to say is all the more genuine. Look here, Mr. Colman, I like you, and I believe you will one day be something more than a gentleman. But that won't do! What's my opinion, good or bad, to you! Listen to me anyhow, and this is what I have to say: you're on the wrong tack here, old boy!"

"I'm sorry, I don't understand you," said Walter.

"Of course not. How could you? But I will explain."

A brief silence followed.

"You heard my story about the ghost?" said Sefton.

"I was about to ask if I might tell it in print."

"You may do what you like with it, except for the other fellow's part."

"Thank you. But I wish you would tell me what you meant by that other more fearful—apparition—or what did you call it? Were you alluding to the ghost?"

"No. There are live women worse than ghosts. Scared as I confess I was, I would rather meet ten such ghosts as I told you of than another woman such as I mean. I know one, and she's enough. By the time you had seen ten ghosts you would have gotten used to them, and found there was no danger from them. But a woman without a soul will devour any number of men. You see she's all empty inside, with plenty of room to devour. But I must be open with you: tell me you are not in love with my cousin Lufa, and my mind will be at peace and I will bid you good night."

"I cannot! I am so much in love with her that I dare not think what may come of it," replied Walter.

"Then for God's sake tell her, and have done with it! Anything will be better than going on like this."

"Why? Whatever are you trying to tell me?" asked Walter with concern in his voice.

"I will not say what Lufa is. Indeed, I don't know what name would fit her at all. I know you probably think me a queer, dry, odd sort of a customer. But I was different when I first fell in love with Lufa. She is older than you think, though not so old as I am. I kept saying to myself she was hardly a woman yet, and that I must give her time. I was better brought up than she. I thought things of importance that she thought none. I didn't have a stupid ordinary mother like hers. She's my second cousin, you know."

Walter nodded, but said nothing.

"She took my words of love, never drew me on, never pushed me back, never refused my love, never returned it. Whatever I did or said, she seemed content. She was always writing poetry. 'But where's her poetry?' I would say to myself. I was always trying to get nearer to what I admired. But she never seemed to suspect the least relation between the ideal and life, between thought and action. To have an ideal implied no aspiration after it in her mind. She never has a thought of the smallest responsibility or obligation to carry out a single one of the fine things she writes of, any more than people that go to church think they have anything to do with what they hear there."

"I do not see how this concerns me," began Walter, but Sefton cut him off with a slight wave of the hand.

"Please, hear me out! You shall have to make up your own mind when I am done. As I was about to say, most people's nature seems all in pieces. They wear and change their moods as they wear and change their dress. Their moods make them, and not they their moods. They are different with every mood. But Lufa seems never to change, and yet never to be in one and the same mood. She is always in two moods, and the one mood has nothing to do with the other. The one mood never influences, never modifies the other. The one mood is enthusiasm for what is not, the other indifference to what *is*. She has no faintest desire to make what is not into what is. For love, I believe all she knows about it is that it is a fine thing to be loved. She loves nobody but her mother, and her only after a fashion. I had my leg broken in the hunting field once. My horse got up and galloped off, and I lay still on the ground. She saw what had happened, and then went off with the hounds. She said she could do no good for me. Dr. Black was in the field, and she went to find him. She didn't find him, though, and he never came. I believe she forgot. But it's worth telling you, though it has nothing to do with her, that I wasn't forgot. My horse, old Truefoot, went straight home, and kept wheeling and tearing up and down in front of the windows, but, till his own groom came, would let no one touch him. Then when he would have led him to the stable, he set his forefeet out in front of him and wouldn't budge. The groom got on his back, but was scarce in the saddle when Truefoot was off in a beeline over everything to where I was lying. Now there's a horse for you! And there's a woman!—I'm telling you all this, mind you, not to blame her, but to warn you. Whether she is to blame or not, I don't know. I don't understand her.

"I was free to come and go here at Comberidge, and say what I pleased. Both families favored the match. I spoke words of love; she never objected, never said she would not have me, said she liked me as well as any other. In a word she would have married me if I would have taken her. I believe there are men who would make the best of such a consent, saying they were so in love with the woman they would rejoice to take her on any terms. But I can't understand that kind of love! I would as soon think of marrying a woman I hated as a woman that did not love me. I know no reason why any woman should love me, and if I can't find one, then I will live out my life alone. Lufa has found no reason to love me yet either, and life and love both seem to be draining out of me in the waiting.

"If you ask me why I do not give it all up, I have no answer. You will say on Lufa's behalf, it is only that the right man for her has not yet come. It may be so. But I can't help believing there is more in it than that. I fear she is all on the outside. It is true that her poetry is even passionate sometimes. But I suspect all her inspiration comes of the poetry she reads, not of the nature or human nature around her. It comes of ambition, not of love. I don't know much about verse, but to me there is an air of artificiality about all hers. I cannot understand how you could praise her long poem so much—if you were in love with her. She has grown to me like the ghost I told you of. I put out my hand to her, and it goes through her. It makes me feel dead myself to be with her. At one time, the ambition filled me to be the one to wake love in her—ambition to be the first and only man so to move her. Despair has long cured me of that, but not before I had come to love her in a way I cannot now understand. Why I should love her I cannot tell; and were it not that I scorn to marry her without love, I should despise my very love.

"You are thinking, 'Well then, the way is clear for me to do my best to win her!' And so it is. There is no one in your way. I only want to prepare you for what I am sure will follow—that you will have the heart taken out of you. Love must be in her somewhere, you will say, otherwise how could she write as she does? But I say again, look at the multitudes that go to church, with whose being the principles of their religion have no more to do with in their daily lives than with that of Satan! I've said my say. Good night."

He rose and stood.

Walter had listened with a beating heart, now full of hope that he was indeed destined to be the one Lufa loved, but then sick with the conviction that he would fare no better than Sefton.

He did not sleep a wink that night. But ever and again across his anxiety, throughout the dark hours, came the flattering thought that the difficulty was not within Lufa at all, but only that she had never loved a man yet, and that he was now teaching her to love.

He did not doubt Sefton, but then Sefton's conclusions might be right only for himself!

19 / The Last Ride

In the morning Walter received a delivery by mail of a copy of his poems that he had taken in sheets to a bookbinder to put in morocco leather for Lady Lufa. Pleased like a child, he handled the volume as if he might hurt it. Such a feeling he had never had before, and would never have again. He was an author!

One might think, after the way in which he had treated not a few books and not a few authors, he could scarcely consider it such a very fine thing to be an author. But there is always a difference between thine and mine, treated by the man of this world as essential. The book was Walter's book and not another's!—no common prose or poetry this, but the firstborn of his deepest feeling! At last it had taken body and shape! From the unseen it had emerged in red morocco, the color of his heart, its edges golden with the light of his hopes!

As to the communication of the night, its pain had nearly vanished. Was not Sefton merely a disappointed lover? His honesty, however, evident, could not alter that fact. Least of all could a man himself tell whether disguised jealousy and lingering hope might not be potently present, while he believed himself solely influenced by friendly concern for another.

"I will take his advice, however," said Walter to himself, "and put an end to my anxiety. I will speak my heart this very day!"

Later, as they sat at the breakfast table, Lufa's voice interrupted Walter's thoughts. "Do you feel inclined for a gallop?" she said. "It feels just like a spring morning. The wind changed in the night. You won't mind a little mud—will you?"

With a commonplace phrase, and foolish look of adoring gratitude, Walter accepted the invitation. Lufa thought he looked handsome as he spoke, and indeed Walter's countenance was not only handsome but expressive. Most women, however, found him attractive chiefly from his frank address and open look, for, though yet far from a true man, he was of a true nature. Every man's nature indeed is true, though the man be not true. But some have come into the world so much nearer the point where they may begin to be true that, comparing them with the rest, we say their nature is true.

Lufa rose and went to get ready. Walter followed and overtook her on the stairs.

"I have something for you," he said. "May I bring it to you in your room?" He could not postpone the effect his book might have. Authors young and old think so much of their books that they seldom conceive how little others care about them.

Lufa nodded her consent and was hardly in her room when he followed with the volume.

She took it, and opened it. "Yours!" she cried. "And poetry! Why, Walter!" She had only once or twice before called him by his first name.

He took it from her hand, and turning the title page, gave it to her again to read the dedication. A slight rose tinge spread over her face. She said nothing, but shut the book and gave it a tender little hug.

"She surely never did that to anything Sefton gave her!" thought Walter.

"Make haste," she said. "I will be down in a moment!" and turning, she went in and closed the door.

Walter went, changed his clothes, and walked up and down the hall for half an hour before she appeared. When she came tripping down the wide, softly descending stairs in her tight-fitting riding habit and hat and feather, holding up her skirt so that he saw her feet racing each other like a little cataract across the steps, saying as she came near him, "I have kept you waiting, but I could not help it; my habit was torn!" he thought he had never seen her so lovely. Indeed she looked lovely, and had she loved, would have been lovely. As it was, her outer loveliness was but a promise whose fulfillment had been too long postponed. Walter's heart swelled into his throat and eyes as he followed her, and helped her to mount her horse.

"Nobody puts me up so well as you," she said.

He could hardly repress the triumph that filled him from head to foot. Whoever might object, she liked him! If she loved him and would confess it, he could live on the pride of it all the rest of his days!

They rode out alone, but neither spoke until they were well beyond the lodge gate. Winter though it was, a sweet air was abroad, and the day was full of spring prophecies: all winters have such days, even those of the heart! How could we get through without them! Their horses were in excellent spirits—it was their first gallop for more than a week; Walter's roan was like a flame under him. The mounts gave them so much to do that no such talk as Walter longed for was possible. It consoled him, however, to think that he had never had such a chance of letting Lufa see he could ride.

At length, after a great long gallop, the two beasts were quieter, seeming to remember they were horses and not colts, and must not overpass the limits of equine propriety.

"Is this our last ride, Lufa?" said Walter.

"Why should it be?" she answered, opening her eyes wide upon him.

"There is no reason I know," he returned, "except—unless you are tired of me."

"Nobody is tired of you—except perhaps George, and you need not mind him. He is odd. I have known him from childhood, and don't understand him yet."

"He is a clever fellow," said Walter.

"I daresay he is—if he would take the trouble to show it."

"I think you hardly do him justice."

"How can I? He bores me! And when I am bored, I am horribly bored. I have been more than patient with him."

"Why do you see him so often then?"

"I don't invite him. Mama is fond of him and so—"

"You are the victim!"

"I can bear it. I have other consolations!"

She laughed merrily.

"How do you like my binding?" he asked when they had ridden a while in silence.

She looked up with a question.

"The binding of my book, I mean," he explained.

"It is a good color."

He felt his hope rather damped.

"Will you let me read a little aloud from it?"

"Of course! You shall have an audience in the drawing room after luncheon."

"Oh, Lufa! How could you think I would read my own poems to a group of people!"

"I beg your pardon. Will the summer house do?"

"Yes, indeed. I can think of nowhere better."

"Very well. The summer house after lunch!"

As they approached the house a few minutes later, Walter said, "Would you mind coming at once to the summer house?"

"But lunch will be ready."

"Then eat in your riding clothes, and come immediately after. Let me have my way for once, Lufa."

"Very well."

20 / The Summer House

The moment the meal was over, Walter left the room, and in five minutes they met at the appointed place—a building like a miniature Roman temple.

"Oh," said Lufa as she entered, "I forgot the book! How stupid of me."

"Never mind," returned Walter. "It was you, not the book, I wanted."

A broad bench went round the circular wall. Lufa seated herself on it, and Walter placed himself beside her, as near as he dared. For some moments he did not speak. She looked up at him inquiringly. He sank at her feet, bowed his head toward her, and but for lack of courage would have laid it on her knees.

"Oh, Lufa!" he said, "you cannot imagine how I love you!"

"Poor, dear boy," she returned, in the tone of a careless mother to whom a son has unburdened his sorrows. She laid her hand lightly on his hair.

The words were not repellent, but neither was the tone encouraging.

"You do not mind my saying it?" he resumed, feeling his way timidly.

"What could you do but tell me?" she answered. "What could I do for you if you did not let me know? I'm *so* sorry, Walter!"

"Why should you be sorry? You can do with me as you please."

"I don't know about such things. I don't quite know what you mean, or what you want. I will be as kind to you as I can—while you stay with us."

"But, Lufa—I may call you Lufa?"

"Yes, of course, if that is any comfort to you."

"Nothing but your love can be a comfort to me. That would make me one of the blessed!"

"I like you very much. If you were a girl, I should say I loved you."

"Why not say it as it is?"

"Would you be content with the love I should give a friend?"

"I will be glad of any love you can give me. But to say I should be *content* with *any* love you could give me would not be true. My love to you is such that I don't know how to bear it. My heart is full of you and longs for you till I can hardly endure the pain. I can never forget you, night or day."

"Then you do try to forget me?"

"Never. Your eyes have so dazzled my soul that I can see nothing else. Do look at me—just for one moment, Lufa."

She turned her face and looked him straight in the eyes— looked into them as if they were windows through which she could peer into the turnings of his brain. She held her eyes steady until his dropped, unable to sustain the nearness of her presence.

"You see," she said, "I am ready to do anything I can to please you."

He felt strangely defeated, rose, and sat down beside her again, with the sickness of a hot summer afternoon in his soul. But he must leave no room for mistake! He had been dreaming long enough.

"Is it possible you do not understand, Lufa, what a man means when he says, 'I love you'?"

"I think I do. I don't mind it!"

"That means you will love me again?"

"Yes, I will be good to you."

"You will love me as a woman loves a man."

"I will let you love me as much as you please."

"To love you as much as I please would be to call you my own, to marry you, to say *wife* to you, to have you completely, with nobody to come between us!"

"Now you are foolish, Walter! You know I never meant that. You must have known that could *never* be! I never imagined you could make such a fantastic blunder! But then, how should *you* know how *we* think about things. I must remember that, and not be too hard on you."

"You mean that your father and mother would not like it?"

"There it is! You do not understand! I thought so. I do not mean my father and mother in particular. I mean our people—people of our position—I would say our *rank,* but that might hurt you. We are brought up so differently from you that you cannot understand how we think of such things. It grieves me to appear unkind, but really, Walter! There is not a man I love more than you—but marriage! Everyone would be talking about *Lady Lufa* the same as if I had run off with my stable groom! Our people are so blind that, believe me, they would hardly see the difference. The idea is simply impossible!"

"It would not be impossible if you loved me!"

"Then I don't, never did, never could love you. Don't imagine you can persuade me to anything unbecoming to my people! You will find yourself awfully mistaken!"

"But I may make a name for myself! If I were to become as famous as Lord Tennyson, would it still be just as impossible?"

"To say it would not would be to confess myself worldly, and that I never was. No, Walter, I admire you. If you could be trusted not to misunderstand, I might even say I loved you. I shall always be glad to see you, always enjoy hearing you read. But beyond that is a line as impassable as the river of death. Say nothing more about it or I must go!"

Here Walter, who had been shivering with cold, began to grow warm again as he answered.

"How could you write that poem—full of such grand things about love, declaring that love is everything and rank nothing—and then, when it comes to yourself, treat me like this! I could not have believed it possible. However much you write about it, I do not think you can know what love is!"

"I hope I never shall if it means any confusion between friendship and folly! Love shall not make a fool of me! I will not be talked about! It's all very well and good in poetry. The idea of letting everything go for love is a splendid idea. It is a pity it should be impossible. There may be some planet, whose social habits are different, where it might work well enough. But here it is not even to be thought of—except in poetry, of course, or in novels. Of all human relations, the idea of such love is certainly the fittest for verse; therefore we have no choice but to use it. But what obligation does my heroine lay on me to behave like her? Why should I fall in love with you in real life because I like to have you read my poem about lovers? Can't you see the absurdity of the argument? Life and books occupy two different spheres. The one is about thoughts, the other about real things, and they don't touch at all."

If it were not for his pride, Walter could have wept with shame. Why should he care that one with such principles should grant or refuse him anything. Yet he could not help caring!

"There is no reason at all why we should not be friends," she resumed. "I am not a flirt, Mr. Colman. It is in my heart to be a sister to you. I would hope that you would be the first to congratulate me when the man appears whom I may choose to love as you mean. He need not be a poet to make you jealous. If he were, I should yet always regard you as my poet."

"And you would let me kiss your shoe, or perhaps your glove, if I was very good!" said Walter.

She took no notice of the outburst; it was but a bit of childish temper.

"You must learn to keep your life and imagination apart," she went on. "You are always letting them mix, and that confuses everything. Of all men, a poet ought not to make that mistake. Poetry is so unlike life that to carry the one into the other is to make the poet a ridiculous parody of a man! The moment that, instead of standing aloof from life and regarding it, he plunges into it, he becomes a traitor to his art and is no longer able to represent things as they ought to be, but cannot be. My mother and I will open to you the best doors in London because we like you. But please do not dream of more."

She had been staring out of the window as she spoke. Now she turned her eyes upon him where he sat, crushed and broken, beside her. A breath of compassion seemed to ruffle the cold lake of her spirit, and she looked at him in silence for a moment. He did not raise his eyes, but her tone made her present to his whole being as she spoke.

"I *don't* want to break your heart, my poet! It was a lovely thought—why did you spoil it?—that we two understood and loved each other in a way nobody could have a right to interfere with."

Walter lifted his head. The word *loved* wrought on him like a spell: he was sadly a creature of words! He looked at her with flushed face and flashing eyes. Often had Lufa thought him handsome, but she had never felt it as she did now.

"Let it be so!" he said. "Be my sister-friend, Lufa. Leave it only to me to remember how foolish I once made myself in your beautiful eyes—how miserable always in my own blind heart."

So little of a man was yet our poet that out of pure disappointment and self-pity, he burst into a passion of weeping. The world seemed lost to him, as it has seemed at such a time to many a better man. But to the true the truth of things will sooner or later assert itself, and neither this world nor the next will prove lost to him. A man's well-being does not depend on any woman. The woman did not create, and could not have contented him. No woman can ruin a man by refusing him, or even by accepting him, though she may go far toward it. There is one who has upon him a perfect claim, at the entrancing recognition of which he will one day cry out, "This, then, is what it all meant!" The lamp of poetry may for a time go out in the heart of the poet, and nature seem a blank. But where the truth is, the poetry must be. And truth *is,* however the untrue may fail to see it. Surely that man is a fool who, on the ground that there cannot be such a God as other fools assert, or such a God as alone he is able to imagine, says there is no God at all!

Lufa's bosom heaved, and she gave a little sighing sob. Her sentiment, the skin of her heart, was touched, for the thing was pathetic! A mist came over her eyes, and might, had she ever wept, have turned to tears.

Walter sat with his head in his hands and wept. She had never before seen a man weep, yet never a tear left its heavenly spring to flow from her eyes! She rose, took his face between her hands, raised it, and kissed him on the forehead.

He rose also, suddenly calmed.

"Then it was our last ride, Lufa!" he said, and left the summer house.

21 / The Drawing Room

When he turned away from Lufa, Walter had no idea where he was going. It was solitude he sought, without being aware that he sought anything.

Must it not be a deep spiritual instinct that drives men and women in trouble into solitude? There are times when only the highest can comfort even the lowest, and solitude is the antechamber to his presence. With our Father is the only possibility of essential comfort, the comfort that turns an evil into a good.

But it was certainly not *knowledge* of this that drove Walter into the wide, lonely park which bordered the garden. "Away from men!" moans the wounded life. Away from the herd flies the wounded deer. Away from the flock staggers the sickly sheep—to the solitary covert to die. The man too thinks he is fleeing in order to die. But it is in truth so to return to life—if indeed he be a man and not an abortion that can console himself with vile consolations. "You cannot soothe me, my friends! Leave me to my misery!" cries the man, and lo his misery is the wind of the waving garments of him who walks in the garden in the cool of the day! All misery is *God unknown*.

Hurt and bleeding Walter wandered away. His life was palled with a sudden hail-cloud which hung low, blotting out color and light and loveliness. It was the afternoon; the sun was fast going down; the dreary north wind had begun again to blow, and the trees to moan in response. They seemed to say, "How sad you are, wind of winter! See how sad you make us! We moan and shiver, each alone, and we are sad!" The sorrow of nature was all about him, but the sighing of the wind-sifting trees around his head and the hardening of the earth about the ancient roots under his feet were better than the glow of the bright drawing room, with its lamps and blazing fires and warm colors. Who could take joy in those with such agony in his heart! He would stay out all night with the suffering, groaning trees that have swallowed the moon and the stars, with the frost and the silent gathering of the companies, troops, and battalions of snow!

Every man understands something of what Walter felt. His soul was seared with cold. The ways of life had become a dull sickness. There was no reason why things should be, why the world should ever have been made! The night was come: why should he keep awake? How cold the river looked in its low, wet channel! How listlessly the long grasses hung over its bank!

It grew darker. He had made a long circle as he walked, and unaware of it was approaching the house. He had not thought about what he must do. Nothing so practical as leaving the place immediately had yet occurred to him. She had not been unkind, he tried to tell himself. She had even pressed on him a sister's love! The moth had not yet burned away enough of its wings to prevent it from burning its whole body; it kept fluttering about the flame! Nor was the childish weakness absent, the unmanly but common impulse, to make the woman feel something of how miserable she had made him. For this poor satisfaction not a few men have blown their brains out; not a few women drowned themselves or taken poison—and generally without success!

Walter would stand before her the ruin she had made him, then vanish from her sight. Tomorrow he would leave the house. But she must see him once more, alone, before he went! Once more he must hang his shrivelled pinions in the presence of the seraph whose radiance had scorched him. And still the most hideous thought of all would keep lifting its vague ugly head out of his chaos—the thought that, lovely as she was, she was not worshipful.

The windows were dimly shining through their thick curtains. The house looked like a great jewel of bliss in which the spirits of paradise might come and go, while such as he could not enter.

Where should he go? To his room and dress for dinner? It was impossible! How could he sit feeling her eyes, and facing Sefton! He could not endure the company, the talk, trying to feign interest in the meal!—all stupid, wearisome, meaningless. No, he would go instead to his room and say he had a headache. But first he would have a quick look into the drawing room: she might be there—and looking sad!

He opened one of the side doors into a corner of the drawing room, looked about, crept in, and closed the door softly behind him.

Lufa was there—alone!

He dared not approach her, but if he seated himself in the corner from which he had entered, he could see her! He did not, however, realize that the particular corner in question was entirely in shadow, or that the lamp was almost straight between them. Therefore, it was impossible that she should be able to see him.

The room seemed to fold him round with softness as he entered from the dreary night. He could not help being pervaded by the warmth and weakened by the bodily comfort. He sat there and gazed at his goddess until he hardly knew whether she was actually in front of him or only present to his thought. She was indeed a little pale—but that was always the case when she was quiet. But no sorrow, not a trace of shadow was on her face. She seemed brooding, but over nothing painful. At length she smiled.

"She is thinking of me," thought Walter. "She is pleased to think that I love her! When the gray hair and wrinkles come, it will be a gracious memory that she was loved by one who had but his life to give her! 'He was poor,' she will say to herself, 'but I have not found the riches he would have given me in anyone else! Ah, to think I let him go! He did indeed love me greatly!' "

For myself, I believe she was thinking instead of a verse that had come to her in the summer house while Walter was weeping by her side.

The main door to the room opened, and Sefton came in.

"Have you seen the *Onlooker*?" he said—a journal at the time much in favor with the more educated populace. "There is a review in it that is very humorous and would amuse you."

"Of what?" she asked listlessly.

"I didn't notice the name of the book, but it is a poem, and just your sort I would say. The article is in the *Onlooker*'s best style, and seems the kind of thing you might enjoy."

"Let me see it," she answered, holding out her hand.

"I will read it to you, if I may."

She did not object. He sat down a little way from her and began to read. He had not gone far before Walter knew, although its title had not occurred as Sefton read, that the book was his own. The discovery enraged him. How had any reviewer got hold of it when he himself had seen no copy except Lufa's! It was a puzzle he never got to the root of, even afterward. Probably someone he had offended with something he had written had contrived to see as much of it at the printer's or binder's as had enabled him to forestall its appearance with the most stinging, mocking, playfully insolent paper that had ever rejoiced the readers of the *Onlooker*. But he had more to complain of than rudeness, a thing of which I doubt any reviewer is ever aware. For he soon found that, by the blunder of the reviewer himself or—horrible thought!—by some blunder of the printer, the best of the verses quoted were misquoted, and so rendered worthy of the disparaging comments attached to them. This unpleasant discovery was presently followed by another—that the rudest and most contemptuous personal remark was founded on an ignorant misapprehension of the reviewer's own; while in ridicule of a mere misprint that happened to carry a comic suggestion on the face of it, the reviewer surpassed himself. In all fairness to whatever reputation Walter may or may not have enjoyed, and notwithstanding that his verse was nothing so great as he himself imagined it, the review was badly misrepresentative both of author and book.

As Sefton read, Lufa laughed often and heartily: the thing was gamesomely, cleverly, wittily, almost brilliantly written. Annoyed as he was, Walter did not fail to note, however, that Sefton did not stop to let Lufa laugh, but read quietly on.

Suddenly a thought seemed to occur to her, and she caught the paper from his hand, for she was quick as a kitten.

"I must see who the author of the precious book is!" she said. Her cousin did not interfere, but sat watching her—almost solemnly.

"Ah, I thought so!" she cried with a shriek of laughter after but a moment. "I could hardly be mistaken! What *will* the poor fellow say to it! It will kill him!"

She laughed immoderately. "I hope it will teach him a lesson, however," she went on. "It is most amusing to see how much he thinks of his own verses! He worships them. And then makes up for the idolatry by handling without mercy those of other people! It was he who so maltreated my poor first book in his own review! I never saw anything so unfair in my life!"

Sefton said nothing, but looked grim.

"You *should* see—I will show it to you—the gorgeous copy of this same comical stuff he gave me today! I am so glad he is leaving. He won't be able to ask me how I like it, and I won't have to lie to him! I'm sorry for him though—truly! He is a very nice sort of boy, though rather presuming. I must find out who the writer of that review is and get Mamma to invite him here. He is a host in himself! I don't think I ever read anything so clever—or more just to its subject!"

"Oh, then you have read the book?" asked her cousin.

"No, but aren't those extracts enough? Don't they speak for themselves—for their silliness and sentimentality?"

"How would you like a book of yours judged by scraps chopped off anywhere, Lufa!—or chosen merely for the look they would have in the humorous frame of the critic's remarks! It is hardly a fair way to review a book. From this review I don't feel I have the least idea what sort of book this is. I only know that many times in the past, after reading a book for myself, I have realized a certain reviewer a knave, who for his own selfish ends did not scruple to make fools of his readers. I am ashamed, Lufa, that you should so accept as gospel everything this reviewer says against a man who believes you are his friend!"

Walter's heart had been as water. Now it turned to ice, and with the coldness came strength: he could bear anything except this desert of a woman. The moment Sefton had thus spoken, he rose and came forward—not so much, I imagine, to Sefton's surprise as Lufa's.

"Thank you, Mr. Sefton," he said, "for undeceiving me. I owe you, Lady Lufa, the debt of a deep distrust hereafter of poetic ladies."

"They will hardly be annihilated by it, Mr. Colman!" returned Lufa. "But, indeed, I did not know you were in the room. Perhaps you did not know that in *our* circle it is counted bad manners to eavesdrop!"

"I was foolishly paralyzed for a moment," said Walter, "as well as unprepared for the part you would take."

"I am very glad, Mr. Colman," said Sefton, "that you have had the opportunity of discovering the truth! My cousin well deserves the pillory in which I know you will now place her."

"Lady Lufa need fear nothing from me. I have some regard left for the idea of her—the thing she is not. If you will be kind enough, come and help me out of the house."

"There is no train tonight."

"I will wait at the station for the slow train in the morning."

"I cannot press you to stay for an hour where you have been so treated," urged Sefton, "but surely—"

"It is high time I left!" said Walter—not without the dignity that endurance gives. "But may I ask you to do one thing for me, Mr. Sefton?"

"Of course—anything!"

"Then please send my portmanteau after me."

With that he left the room and went to his own on his way to the curing of his heart, though not quite so far as he imagined. The blood, however, was surging healthily through his veins. He had been made a fool of, but he would be a wiser man for it!

He had hardly arrived when Sefton appeared. "Would you like some help?" he said.

"To pack my portmanteau?" replied Walter. "Did you ever pack your own?"

"You think we of the aristocracy so helpless? Yes, I've packed my own oftener than you may think! I never had but one orderly I could bear to keep about me, and he's dead, poor fellow. I shall see him again, though, I do trust. Never will I cease hoping to see my old Archie again! Fellows must learn something through the Lufas, or they would make raving maniacs of us! God be thanked, he has her in his great idiot cage, and will do something with her yet! May you and I be there to see when she comes out in her right mind."

"Amen!" said Walter.

"And now, my dear fellow," said Sefton, "if you will listen to me, you will not need to go before tomorrow morning.—But no, I don't suppose it would do to have you stay to breakfast! You shall go by the early train as any other visitor might. The least scrap of a note to Lady Tremaine, and all will go without so much as a remark."

He waited in silence as Walter continued to pack his things.

"I daresay you are right!" said Walter after a moment. "I will stay till the morning. But you will not ask me to go downstairs to join them again?"

"It would be a victory for you if you could."

"Very well, I will. I am a fool, but this much less of a fool, that at last I know I am one."

Somehow a sense of relief came over Walter. He began to dress for dinner and spent some pains on the process. He felt sure Sefton would take care that the copy of the *Onlooker* should not be seen—before his departure, anyhow.

During dinner he talked cheerfully, almost brilliantly, making Lufa open her eyes without knowing she did.

He retired again to his room much later in the evening, with very mixed feelings. Here was the closing paragraph of the most interesting chapter of his life yet constructed. What was to follow, he wondered.

> Into the gulf of an empty heart
>   Something must always come!
> "What will it be?" I think with a start,
>   And a fear that makes me dumb.

> I cannot sit at my outer gate
>> And call what shall soothe my grief;
> I cannot unlock to a king in state,
>> Cannot bar a wind-swept leaf!
>
> Hopeless were I if a loving Care
>> Sat not at the spring of my thought—
> At the birth of my history, blank and bare,
>> Of the thing I have not wrought.
>
> If God were not, this hollow need,
>> All that I now call *me,*
> Might wallow with demons of hate and greed
>> In a lawless and shoreless sea!
>
> Watch the door of this sepulchre,
>> Sit, my Lord, on the stone,
> Till the life within it rise and stir,
>> And walk forth to claim its own.

This was how Walter felt, and these were the words he wrote some twelve months afterward, when he had come to understand a little of the process that had been conducted in him; when he knew that the life he had been living was a mere life in death, a being not worth being.

But the knowledge of this process had not yet begun. A thousand subtle influences, wrapped in the tattered cloak of dull old Time, had to come into secret, potent play before he would be able to write thus.

And even this paragraph of his life was not yet quite, as he thought, at an end.

22 / A Midnight Interview

Walter drew his table near the fire and sat down to concoct a brief note of thanks and farewell to his hostess, informing her that he was compelled to leave abruptly. He found it rather difficult, though what Lufa might tell her mother he neither thought nor cared. If only he had his back to the house, and his soul out of it. It was now the one place on the earth that he would sink in the abyss of forgetfulness.

He could not get the note to come out as he wanted it, falling constantly into thought after thought that led nowhere. At last he threw himself back in his chair, wearied with the emotions of the day. Under the soothing influence of the heat and the lambent motions of the flames, he fell into a condition that was not sleep, but was just as little to be called wakefulness. His childhood crept back to him, with all the delights of the sacred time when home was the universe, and father and mother the divinities that filled it. A something now vanished from his life, looked at him across a gulf of lapse, and said, "Am I likewise false? The present you desire to forget. You say it would be better if it had never been. Do you wish I too had never been? Why else have you left my soul in the grave of oblivion." And thus talking with his past, he fell asleep.

It could have been but for a few minutes, though when he woke it seemed a century had passed, he had dreamed of so much. But something had happened! What was it? The fire was blazing as before, but he was chilled to the very marrow of his bone! A wind seemed blowing upon him, cold as if it came from the very jaws of the sepulchre! His imagination and memory together linked the time to the night of Sefton's warning: was the ghost now come to visit him? Had Sefton's presence only saved him from her for the time?

He sat bolt upright in his chair listening, the same horror filling him as it had then.

It seemed long minutes he thus sat motionless, but moments of fearful expectation are long drawn out; their nature is of centuries, not years. One thing was certain, and only one—there was indeed a wind, and a very cold one, blowing upon him.

He stared at the door. It moved. It opened a little. A light tap followed. Walter was paralyzed and could not speak for fear. Then came a louder tap, and at once the spell was broken. He jumped to his feet, and with the courage of extreme terror, opened the door—not just a crack, as if he feared an unwelcome human presence, but pulled it open wide with a sudden swing.

There stood no bodiless soul, but soulless Lufa!

He stood aside, and invited her to enter. Little as he desired to see her, it was a relief that it was she, and not an elderly lady in brown silk, through whose person you might thrust your hand without injury or offense.

As a reward of his promptitude in opening the door, he caught sight of Lady Tremaine disappearing in the corridor.

Lady Lufa walked in without a word, and Walter followed her, leaving the door wide open. She seated herself in the chair he had just left, and turned to him with a quiet, magisterial air, as if she sat on the seat of judgment.

"You had better shut the door," she said.

"I thought Lady Tremaine might wish to hear," answered Walter.

"Not at all. She only helped me to the door with the light of her candle."

"As you please," said Walter, and having done as she requested, returned, and stood before her.

"Will you not take a seat?" she said, in the tone of "You may sit down."

"Your ladyship will excuse me," he answered, "I will remain where I am."

She gave a condescending motion to her pretty neck, and said, "I need hardly explain, Mr. Colman, why I have sought this interview. You must by this time be aware how peculiar, indeed, how unreasonable your behavior was."

"I do not see the necessity for a word on the matter. I plan to leave by the first train in the morning."

"I will not dwell on the rudeness of listening—"

"To a review of my own book read by a friend!" interrupted Walter with indignation, "in a drawing room where I sat right in front of you, and knew no reason why you should not see me! I did make a great mistake, but it was in trusting a lady who, an hour or two before, had offered to be my sister! How could I suspect she might speak of me in a way she would not like me to hear!"

Lady Lufa was not quite prepared for the tone he took. She had expected to find him easy to cow. Her object was to bring him into humble acceptance of the treatment against which he had rebelled, lest he should afterward avenge himself via the printed page. She sat a moment in silence.

"Such ignorance of the ways of the world," she finally said, "is excusable in a poet—especially—"

"Such a poet!" supplemented Walter, who found it difficult to keep his temper in face of her arrogance.

"But the world is made up of those who laugh and those who are laughed at."

"They change places, however, sometimes!" said Walter—which alarmed Lufa, though she did not show her anxiety.

"Certainly," she replied. "Everybody laughs at everybody else when he gets a chance. What is society but a club for mutual criticism. The business of its members is to pass judgment on each other. Why not take this little misunderstanding, which seems so to annoy you, with the philosophy of a gentleman—like one of us! None of us think anything of what is said of us; we do not heed what we say of each other! Everyone knows that all his friends pull him to pieces the moment he is out of sight—as heartily as they had just been assisting him to pull others to pieces.

Every gathering is a temporary committee, composed of those who are present and sitting upon those who are not. Nobody dreams of courtesy extending beyond one's presence! Only the most inexperienced person could suppose that things going on in his absence are the same as when he is present. It is I who ought to be pitied as being part of such a system, not you!"

Walter bowed and was silent. He did not yet see her drift.

With sudden change of tone and expression, she broke out: "Be generous, Walter! Forgive me. I will make any atonement you please, and never again speak of you as if you were not my own brother!"

"It is not of consequence how you speak of me now, Lady Lufa. I have had the painful good fortune to learn your real feelings, and prefer the truth to the most agreeable deception. Your worst opinion of me I could have borne and loved you still. But there is nothing left in a sweet but false woman to love."

"Well, you are ungenerous! I hope there are not many in the world to whom one might confess a fault and not be forgiven. This is indeed humiliating!"

"I'm sorry; I heard no confession."

"I asked you to forgive me."

"For what?"

"For talking of you as I did."

"Which you did not repent of as a wrong, but rather justified as the custom of society."

"I confess, then, that in your case I ought not to have done so."

"Then I forgive you, and we part in peace."

"Is that what you call forgiveness?"

"Is that what *you* call repentance? I have said I forgive you. I see nothing more that is required beyond that between the merest of acquaintances."

"It is terrible to have such an enemy!"

"I do not understand you."

"The fight is not fair! Here I stand—poor, undefended,

chained to the rock of my name and position. There you lurk—
behind the hedge, invisible, taking every advantage of me! Do
you think it is fair?"

"Ah, now I think I begin to understand you. Your objection
did not seem to strike you while *I* was the person being shot at
by your words! But still I fail to see your object."

"You *must* know perfectly well what I mean, Walter! And I
cannot but believe you mean to allow a personal misunderstanding
to influence your public judgment of me. You gave your real
unbiased opinion of my last book, and you are bound by that!"

"Is it possible that at last I understand you!" cried Walter.
"That you should come to me on such an errand, Lady Lufa,
reveals yet more your opinion of me! *Could* you possibly believe
me capable of such meanness as to take my revenge by abusing
your work in my review?"

"Ah, no . . . of course not!—Promise me you will not."

"If such a promise were necessary, how could it ease your
mind? The man who could do such a thing would break any
promise."

"If you will *not* promise, then I shall take whatever rudeness
is offered toward me in your journal as springing from your personal resentment!"

"If you do, you will wrong me far worse than you have yet
done. I shall not merely never again review a work of yours, I
will never utter an opinion of it to any man or woman."

"Thank you. So we part friends."

"Conventionally."

She rose. He turned to the door and opened it. She passed
him, her head thrown back, her eyes looking poisonous, and let
a gaze of contemptuous doubt rest on him for a moment. His eyes
did not quail before hers.

She had left a candle taper burning on a slab outside the door.
Walter had but half closed it behind her when she reappeared with
the taper in one hand and the volume he had given her in the
other. He took the book without a word, and again she went; but
he had hardly thrown it on the hot coals when once more she

appeared. I believe she herself had blown her candle out for an excuse to reenter.

"Let me have a light, please," she said.

He took the taper from her hand and turned to light it. She followed him into the room and laid her hand on his arm.

"Walter," she said, "it was all because of Sefton! He does not like you, and can't bear me to like you! I am engaged to him. I ought to have told you."

"I will congratulate him next time I see him!" said Walter.

"No, no!" she cried, looking at once both angry and scared.

"Then I will not," answered Walter. "But allow me to say I do not believe Sefton dislikes me. Anyhow, keep your mind at ease. I shall certainly not in any way avenge myself."

She looked up in his eyes with a momentary glimmer of her old sweetness, said "Thank you!" gently, and left the room. Her last glance left a faint, sad sting in Walter's heart, and he began to think whether he had been too hard upon her. In any case, the sooner he was out of the house, the better! He must no more trifle with the girl than an alcoholic with a brandy bottle!

All during their last brief interchange, the gorgeous book was frizzling and curling and cracking on the embers. Whether she saw it or not I cannot say, but she was followed all along the corridor by the smell of the burning leather, which got into some sleeping noses, and made their owners dream the house was on fire.

In the morning, Sefton woke him, helped him to dress, got him away in time, and went with him to the station. Not a word passed between them about Lufa. All the way to London Walter pondered whether there could be any reality in what she had said about Sefton. Was it not possible that she might have imagined him jealous? Sefton's dislike of her treatment of him might to her have seemed displeasure at her familiarity with him! *And indeed,* thought Walter, *there are few friends who care so much for any author, I suspect, as to be indignant with his reviewers!*

23 / An Evening at the Theater, and Its Result

If London had been dreary when Lufa left, it was worse than dreary to Walter now that she was gone from his world, gone from the universe past and future both—for the Lufa he had dreamed of was not, and had never been!

He no longer had anyone to dream about, waking or asleep. The space she had occupied was a blank spot, black and cold, charred with the fire of passion, cracked with the frost of disappointment and scorn. It had its intellectual trouble too—the impossibility of bringing together the long cherished *idea* of Lufa, and the *reality* of Lufa as revealed by herself. Now also he had no book to occupy him with pleasant labor. It had passed from him into the dark; the thought of it was painful, almost loathsome to him. He was glad, however, that none of his associates referred to it. His friends pitied him, and his foes were silent. Three copies of the book were sold. The sneaking review Sefton had stumbled across had enough influence with the public to utterly annihilate any chance it might have had.

But the expenses of printing remained. He still had to pay his share of them. And alas, he did not know where any money was to come from! The publisher would give him time, no doubt, but it would take years even working his hardest. Besides this, there was also the shame of having undertaken what he was unable at once to fulfill. He set himself to grind on and starve.

At times the clouds would close in upon him, and there would seem nothing worth living for; though in truth his life was now all the more valuable that Lufa was out of it. Occasionally his heart would grow very gentle toward her, and he would burrow about in his mind for some possible way to excuse her. But his conclusion was always the same: how could he ever forget that laugh of utter merriment and delight when she found it was indeed himself under the castigation of such a mighty beadle of literature! In his most melting mood, therefore, he could only pity her.

Yet what might have become of him had she not thus unmasked herself! He would now be believing her the truest, best of women, with no fault but a coldness of which he had no right to complain, a coldness comforted by the extent of its freezing.

But there was far more to make London miserable to him: he had now at last become disgusted with his trade. This continuous feeding on the labor of others was no work for a gentleman! He began to see in it certain analogies that grew more and more unpleasant as he regarded them. He was also sick of his own poetizing. True, the quality or value of what he had written was not in any way itself affected by its failure to meet acceptance. It had certainly not had fair play. But now that the blinding influence of their chief subject was removed, he saw the verses themselves to be of little worth. The soul of them was not the grand all-informing love but his own private self-seeking little passion for a poor show of the lovable. No one could possibly care for such verses, except indeed it was some dumb soul in love with a woman like the woman of their thin worship! Some of the verses may have been pretty, some quaint, but throughout there was no revelation. He had put on his singing robes to whisper his secret love into the ears of the public—desiring recognition, fame, and a good report. That he had not received it, he said to himself, was better than he deserved!

What now could life be to lie wallowing among the mushrooms of the press! To spend whatever gifts he had merely in saying that this man had done well, that another had done ill, that so-and-so was amusing, and that she was dull—was such to be called worthwhile work? His conscience, his taste, his desires could not support him in such labor any longer. What was he doing for the world? they asked him. How many books had he guided men to read, by whose help they might steer their way through the shoals of life?

He could count on the fingers of one hand the books he had heartily recommended. If he had but pointed out what was good in books otherwise poor, it would have been something! But alas! his had been the pen of critique, the pen of his own thoughts. He had not found it easy to be at once clever, honest, and serviceable to his race: the press was but for the utterance of opinion, true or false, not for the education of thought. And why should such as he write books, who had nothing to tell men that could make them braver, stronger, purer, more loving, less selfish!

But what was to be done? He must work, yet his calling to literature had vanished! He owed his landlady money. He must eat. There must be *something* honest for him to do!

The true Walter was waking slowly at last—beginning to see things as they were and not as men regarded them. He was tormented with doubts and fears of all kinds. But for the change in his father's financial circumstances, he would have asked for his help at once. And had he been truer to his father, he would have known that such a decision would even now have rejoiced the old man's heart.

He no longer possessed enough confidence within himself to write on any social question. Of the books sent him for review, he chose such as seemed worthiest of notice, but could not do much. He felt not merely a growing disinclination, but a growing incapacity for the work, and as he was paid by the article, his income continued to dwindle in proportion to his shrinking output. How much the feeling may have been increased by the fact that his health was giving way, I cannot tell. But certainly the root of both problems was moral.

His funds began to fail his immediate necessities. He had just come from pawning the watch which he would have sold but that it had been his mother's and was the gift of his father when he met his friend Harold Sullivan, who persuaded him to accompany him to the theater. Between the first and second acts, he caught sight of Lady Lufa in one of the boxes, with Sefton standing behind her. There was hardly a chance of their seeing him, and he watched them at his ease, glad to see Sefton, and not sorry to see Lufa, for it was an opportunity of testing himself.

He could see that they held almost no communication with each other, but was not surprised, knowing the peculiar relation in which they stood. Lufa was not looking unhappy—far from it; her countenance expressed absolute self-contentment. Sefton's look was certainly not one of contentment, but neither was it exactly one of discontent. It suggested power awaiting opportunity, strength quietly attendant upon, hardly expectant of the moment of activity. Walter imagined one watching a beloved cataleptic: till she came alive, what was to be done but wait? God has had more waiting than anyone else. Lufa was an iceberg that would not melt even in the warm southward sea, watched by a still volcano, whose fires were of no avail, for they could not reach her.

Now and then a soft sadness would for a moment settle on Sefton's face—like the gray of a cloudy summer evening about to gather into a warm rain. But this was never when he looked at her; it was only when, without seeing, he thought about her. Up till now Walter had not been capable of understanding the devotion, the quiet strength, the persistent purpose of the man. Now he began to see into it and admire him all the more. While a spark of hope lay alive in those ashes of disappointment that had often seemed as if they would make but a dust heap of his bosom, there he must remain, by the clean, cold hearth, swept and garnished, of the woman he loved—loved strangely, mysteriously, inexplicably even to himself!

Walter sat gazing at them, and as he gazed, simultaneously the two became aware of his presence. A friendly smile spread over Sefton's face. To Walter's wonder, perfectly self-contained and unchangingly self-obedient Lufa colored—faintly indeed, but plainly enough to the eyes of one so well used to the white rose of her countenance. She moved neither head nor body, only turned her eyes away, and seemed, like the dove for its foot, to seek some resting place for her vision.

And with the sight awoke in Walter the first unselfish resolve of his life. Might he not be able to do something to bring those two together?

The thought seemed even to himself almost a foolish one. But spiritual relations and potencies go far beyond intellectual ones, and a man must become a fool to be wise. Many a foolish thought, many an improbable idea, has proved itself seed-bearing fruit of the kingdom of heaven. A man may fail to effect, or be able to set hand to work he would like to do—and yet be judged by what he *would* have done if he could. Only the *would* must be as true as a deed; then it *is* a deed. The kingdom of heaven is for the dreamers of true dreams only!

Was there then anything Walter could do to help the man gain the woman he had so faithfully helped Walter to lose? It was no ordinary task. The thing was not to enable him to marry her—that Sefton could have done long ago, and could do any day without anyone's help. But as Lufa then was, she was no gain for any true man! But was there any way he could help open the eyes of the conceited, foolish girl, either to her own valuelessness as she was, or to her worth as she might be, or again to the value, the eternal treasure of the heart she was turning from? If he could do something—anything!—then indeed would she be a gift that in the giving grew worthy even of such a man!

With such questions came a reflection that had not occurred to Walter before. In nothing are we slower than in discovering our own blame—and the slower that we are so quick to perceive or imagine we perceive the blame of others. For the very fact that we see and heartily condemn the faults of others, we use, unconsciously perhaps, as an argument that we must ourselves be right. We must take heed not to judge with the idea that so we shall escape judgment—that by condemning evil we clear ourselves. For indeed, we are told just the opposite, that by such judgment, we will come under judgment ourselves! And now Walter's eyes were opened to see that he had done Lufa a great wrong; that he had helped immensely to buttress and exalt her self-esteem.

Had he not in his whole behavior toward her been far more anxious that he should please her than that she should be worthy? Had he not known that she was far more anxious to be accepted as a poet than to be admired as a woman?—more anxious indeed to be accepted than, even in the matter of her art, to be worthy of acceptance—to be the thing she wished to be thought of? In that review which, in spite of his own soul, he had persuaded himself to publish, knowing it to be false, had he not actively, most unconscientiously, and altogether selfishly, done her serious intellectual wrong and heavy moral injury? Was he not bound to make what poor reparation might be possible?

It mattered nothing that she did not desire any such reparation. Indeed, she would no doubt look upon anything he did as a pretense for the sake of insult and the revenge of giving her pain. Yet having told her the lies, he must confess they were lies. Having given her the poison of falsehood, he must at least follow it with the only antidote: the truth! It was not his part to determine consequences, so long as a duty remained to be done. And what could be more a duty than to undeceive where he had deceived, especially where the deception was aggravating that worst of all human diseases: self-conceit, self-satisfaction, and self-worship.

It was doubtful whether she would read what he might write, but the fact that she did not trust him, and that, notwithstanding his assurance, she would still be afraid of his public criticism of her work, would, he thought, secure for him at least a reading of what he might attempt to say to her. She might in the end destroy the letter in disgust. But he would have done what he could. He had begun to turn a new leaf, and here was a thing the new leaf required written upon it!

As for Sefton, what better thing could he do for him than make Lufa think less of herself? Or, if such was impossible, at least make her understand that other people did not think so much of her as she had willingly been led to believe! In wronging her he had wronged his friend as well, throwing obstacles in the way of his reception. He had wronged the truth itself!

When the play was over and the crowd was dispersing, he found himself close to them on the pavement as they waited for their carriage. But what a change had passed on him! Not once did he find himself wishing her to look round at him, and he kept silent. Sefton, moved perhaps by that unknown power of presence, operating in bodily proximity but savoring of the spiritual, looked suddenly round and saw him. He smiled and did not speak, but stretching out a quiet hand, sought his. Walter grasped it and they clasped in a firm shake. Lufa knew nothing beyond the swaying human flood.

Having made up his mind on the way, he set to work as soon as he reached home. He wrote and destroyed and rewrote, erased and substituted, until, as near as he could, he had said what he intended, so at least as it should not be mistaken for what he did not intend, which is the main problem in writing. Then he copied everything out fair and plain, so that she could read it easily—and here is his letter, word for word:

MY DEAR LADY LUFA,

In part by means of the severe lesson I received through you, a great change has passed upon me. I am no longer able to think of myself as the important person I used to take myself for. It is startling to have one's eyes opened to see oneself as one is, but it very soon begins to make one glad, and the gladness, I find, goes on growing.

One's nature is so elevated by being delivered from the honoring and valuing of that which is neither honorable nor valuable that the seeming loss is annihilated by the essential gain. Being better makes up infinitely for showing to myself worse. I would millions of times rather know myself a fool than imagine myself a great poet. For to know oneself a fool is to begin to be wise; and I would be loyal among the sane, not royal among lunatics! Who would be the highest, in virtue of the largest mistake, of the profoundest self-idolatry!

But it was not to tell you this that I began to write. It was to confess a great wrong which I once did you. For I cannot rest, I cannot make it up with my conscience until I have told you the truth. It may be you will dislike me all the more for confessing the wrong than for committing it in the first place—I cannot tell. But it is my part to let you know it—and nonetheless my part that I must therein confess myself more weak and foolish than I already appear.

You will remember that you gave me a copy of your drama while I was at your house: the review of it which appeared in the *Battery* I wrote that same night. I am ashamed to have to confess the fact, but I had taken more champagne than, I hope, I ever shall again. And, irreverent as it must seem to mention the fact in such a connection, I was possessed almost to insanity with your beauty and the graciousness of your behavior to me. Everything around me was pervaded with rose color and rose odor, and my head and heart, my imagination and senses, my memory and hope were all full of yourself when I sat down to read your poem. I was like one in an opium dream. I saw everything in the glory of an everlasting sunset; for every word I read, I heard in the tones of your voice. The radiant consciousness of your beauty thoroughly received every thought that awoke. If ever one being was possessed by another, I was that night possessed by you. In this mood, like that, I say again, brought on by some drug, I wrote the review of your book.

But on the morning after the writing of it, I found, when I began to read it, I could so little enter into the feeling of it that I could hardly believe I had actually written what lay before me in my own hand. I took the poem again and scanned it most carefully, reading it with deep, anxious desire to justify the things I had set down. But I failed altogether. Even my love could not blind me enough to persuade me that what I had said was true, or that I should be other than false to print it. I had to put myself through a succession of special pleadings before I could quiet my conscience enough to let the thing go off in the mail and tell its lies in the ears of the disciples of the *Battery*.

I will show you how falsely I dealt. I said to myself that, in the first place, one mood had, in itself, as good a claim with regard to the worth of what it produced as another; but that the opinion of the night, when the imagination was awake, was actually more likely to be just with regard to a poem than that of the cold, hard, unpoetic day. I was wrong in taking it for granted that my moods had equal claims; and the worse wrong—that all the time I knew I was not behaving honestly, for I persisted in leaving out, as a factor in one of the moods, the champagne I had drunk, not to mention the time of the night and the glamour of your influence. The latter was still present the next morning, but could no longer blind me to believe what I would—most of all things—have gladly believed. With the mood the judgment was altered, and a true judgment is the same in all moods, inhabiting a region above mood.

In confession, a man must use plain words: I was a coward, a false friend, a false man. Having tried my hardest to keep myself from seeing the fact as plainly as I might had I looked it in the face with the intent of meeting what the truth might render necessary, yet knowing that I was acting falsely, I sent it off, regardless of duty, in the sole desire of pleasing you, and had printed, as my opinion concerning your book, what was not my opinion. For the oftener I read thereafter, the more I was convinced that I had given such an opinion as must stamp me the most incompetent, or the falsest of critics.

Lady Lufa, there is nothing remarkable in your poem. It is nicely, correctly written, and in parts skillfully contrived. But had it been sent me among other books, and without indication of the author, I should have dismissed it as the attempt of a schoolgirl who happened to have sufficient money to print it.

You may say this judgment is the outcome of my jealous disappointment. I would say rather that the former was the outcome of my loving fascination. And I cannot but think something in yourself will speak for me and tell you that I am speaking honestly. Mr. Sefton considers me worthy of belief. And I know myself worthier of belief than ever before—how much worthier than when I wrote that review! Then I loved you—selfishly. Now I love the truth, and would serve you, though I do not love you the same way as before. Through the disappointment you caused me, my eyes have been opened to see the way in which I was going, and to turn from it; for I was walking along the path of falsehood.

Oh, Lady Lufa, let me speak! Forget my presumption! You bore with my folly—please bear now with what is true, though it come from a foolish heart! What would it be to us if we gained the praises of the whole world and found afterward they were empty praises for what was counted of no value in the great universe into which we had passed? Let us be true, whatever come of it, and look the facts of things in the face.

If I am a poor creature, let me be content to know it; for in that knowledge, do I not have the joy that God can make me great? And is not the first step toward greatness to refuse to call that great which is not great, or to think myself great when I am small? Is it not an essential and impassable bar to greatness for a man to imagine himself great when there is not in him one single element of greatness? Let us confess ourselves that which we cannot consent to remain! The confession of not being is the sole foundation for becoming. Self is a quicksand! God is the only rock! I have been learning a little.

Having dared to say all these things to you, why should I not go further and say one thing more that is burning within me! There was a time when I might have said it better in verse, but that time has gone by—to come again, I trust, when I have that to say which is worth saying; when I shall be true enough to help my fellows to be true. The calling of a poet, if it be a calling, must come from heaven. To be bred to a thing is to have the ears closed to any call.

There is a man I know who forever sits watching, as one might watch in the evening for the first star to come creeping out of the infinite heaven. But it is for a higher and lovelier star this man watches. He is waiting for a woman, for the first dawn of her soul. He knows well the spot where the star of his hope must appear, the spot where, out of the vast unknown, she must open her shining eyes that he may love her.

But alas, she will not rise and shine. He believes or at least hopes his star is on the way, and what can he do but wait, for he is laden with

the burden of a wealth given him to give—the love of a true heart—
the rarest, as the most precious thing on the face of this half-baked
brick of a world.

It was easy for me to love you, Lady Lufa, while I took that for
granted in you which did not exist in myself. But he knows the truth
of you, and yet loves you! Lady Lufa, you are not yet true. If you do
not know it, it is because you will not know it, lest the sight of your
incomplete being should unendurably urge you toward that which you
will not choose to be. God is my witness, I speak from no anger or
jealousy! Not a word I say is for myself! I am but begging you to
become that which God, in making you, intended you to be. I would
have the star shine through the cloud—shine on the heart of the watcher!
The real Lufa lies hidden under a dusky garment. None but God can
see through to the lovely thing he made, out of which the unreal Lufa
is smothering the life. When the beautiful child, the real Lufa, the
person you know you ought to be, walks out like an angel from a grave,
then will the heart of God, and the heart of George Sefton, rejoice with
a great joy!

Think what the love of such a man is. It is your very self he loves.
He loves like God, even before the real self has begun to exist. It is
not the beauty you show but the beauty showing you that he loves—
the hidden self of your perfect idea. Outward beauty alone is not for
the divine lover; it is a mere show. Until the woman makes it real, it
is but a show; and until she makes it true, she is herself untrue. With
you, Lady Lufa, it rests to make your beauty a truth, that is, a divine
fact.

For myself, I have been but a false poet—a mask among poets, a
builder with hay and stubble, babbling before I had words, singing
before I had a song, without a ray of revelation from the world unseen,
carving at clay instead of shaping it in the hope of marble. I am humbler
now, and trust the divine humility has begun to work out mine. Of all
things I would be true, and pretend nothing.

Lady Lufa, if a woman's shadow came out of her mirror and went
about the world pretending to be the woman herself, that figure thus
walking the world and stealing hearts would be like you. Would to God
I were such an exorcist as could lay that ghost of you! as could say,
"Go back, forsake your seeming, false image of the true, the lovely
Lufa that God made! You are but her unmaking! Get back into the
mirror, and leave the true Lufa to awake from the swoon into which
you have cast her! She must live and grow and become till she is perfect
in loveliness."

I shall know nothing of the fate of my words. I doubt I shall see
you again in this world—except it be by accident as I saw you tonight
at the theater. But the man who loves you sees the sleeping beauty

within you! His lips are silent, yet by the very silence of his lips his love speaks. But if we are true, we shall meet again and have much to say. If we are not true, all we know is that falsehood must perish.

For me, I will arise and go to my father, and lie no more. I will be a man, and live in the truth—try at least so to live, in the hope of one day being true.

Walter Colman

Walter sent the letter—posted it the next morning as he went to the office. It has been many years since that day, and he has not heard of it yet. But there is nothing hidden that shall not be revealed.

The writing of this letter was a great strain, both emotionally and physically, to him, but he felt much relieved when it was gone. How differently he felt after that other lying, flattering utterance, with his half-sleeping conscience muttering and grumbling as it lay. He walked then full of pride and hope, in the midst of his dream of love and ambition. Now he was poor and sad, and bowed down, but the earth was a place that might be lived in despite such feelings. If only he could find some thoroughly honest work! He would rather have his weakness and dejection with his humility than ten times the false pride with which he paced the street before.

But the effort had taxed his already weakened condition more than he knew, and he came home that night far from well and altogether incapable of work. He was indeed ill, for he could neither eat nor sleep nor concentrate on anything. His friend Sullivan was shocked to see him looking so pale, and insisted he must go home. Walter said it was no doubt just a passing attack of something, and he would not want to alarm them; he would wait a day or two.

At length he felt so sick that one morning he did not get out of bed. There was no one in the apartment house to nurse him; his landlady did little or nothing for him beyond getting him the cup of tea he occasionally wanted. Sullivan himself became ill, and for some days neither saw nor heard from the other. During that time Walter had such an experience of loneliness and desertion as he had never had before. But it was a purgatorial suffering.

He began to learn how insufficient he was for himself, how little sustaining power there was in him. There was no fountain of life in his soul!

Words that had been mere platitudes of theological commonplace began to show a golden root through their ancient mold. The time came back to him when father and mother bent anxiously over their child. He remembered how their love took from him all fear, how even the pain seemed to melt in their presence. All was right when they knew all about it! They would see that the suffering went at the proper time! All gentle ministrations to his comfort—the moving of his pillows, the things cooked by his mother's own hands, her watch to play with—a multitude of memories came back to him as if the tide of life had set to moving in the other direction, and he was fast drifting back into childhood. What sleep he had was filled with alternate dreams of suffering and home deliverance. He recalled how different his aunt had been when he was sick: in this isolation her face looking in at his door would have been as that of an angel!

All the time as he lay, he knew that his debts were increasing, and he had no idea when he would be capable of beginning to pay them off! His mind wandered, and when Sullivan came to visit him again at length, he was talking wildly, imagining himself the prodigal son in the parable.

Sullivan wrote at once to Mr. Colman.

24 / To London!

It was during the afternoon when Sullivan's letter arrived, on the lower left-hand corner of which he had written *Har. Sul.* Mr. Colman had gone for the day to a town some distance away, and would not be back until the last train late in the evening. He did not receive much mail, and this particular letter, with the London postmark, naturally drew the immediate attention of Aunt Ann and Molly. The moment the eyes of the former fell on the abbreviated name in the corner, they blazed.

"The shameless fellow!" she cried, "—writing to beg another ten-pound note from my poor foolish brother!"

"I don't think that is it, Auntie," returned Molly.

"And why not? How should you know?"

"Mr. Sullivan has had plenty of work, and cannot need to borrow money. Why are you so suspicious, Auntie?"

"I am not. I never was suspicious. You are a rude girl to say so! If it is not money, you may depend upon it, it is something worse!"

"What worse can you mean?"

"That Walter has got into some scrape?"

"If that were so, why would he not write himself?"

"He is probably too much ashamed, and gets his friend to do it for him. I know the ways of young men!"

"Perhaps he is ill," said Molly.

"Perhaps. It is a long time since I saw a letter from him. I am never allowed to read a single one of them!"

"Can you wonder at that when you are always abusing him? If he were my son, I should take care you never saw a scrap of

his writing! It upsets me to hear those I love talked of as you talk
of him—always with a sniff!"

"Love, indeed! Do you suppose no one loves him but you?"

"His father loves him dearly."

"How dare you hint that I do not love him!"

"If yours is love, Auntie, I wish I may never meet it where
I've no chance of defending myself!"

Molly had a hot temper where her friends were concerned,
though she would bear a good deal without retorting.

"There," said Aunt Ann, giving her the letter; "put that on
the mantlepiece till my brother comes."

Molly took it, and gazed wistfully at it, as if trying to read it
through the envelope. She had that morning had a strange and
painful dream about Walter—that he lay in his coffin with a white
cat across his face.

"What if he *should* be ill, Auntie?" she said.

"Who?"

"Walter, of course!"

"What of it? We must wait to know."

"Father wouldn't mind if we just opened it to make sure it
was not about Walter."

"Open my brother's letter! Gracious, what next! Well, you
are a girl! I should just like to see him after you had opened one
of his letters!"

Miss Hancock herself had once done so—out of pure curi-
osity, though on another pretense—a letter, as it happened, which
Mr. Colman would rather not have read himself than have had
her read, for it contained thanks for a favor secretly done, and
upon learning of his sister-in-law's action was more angry than
anyone had ever seen him. Molly remembered the occurrence,
though she had been too young to have it explained to her. But
Molly's idea of a father, and of Richard Colman as that father,
was much grander than that of most children concerning fathers.
There is indeed a much closer relation between some good men
and any good child than there is between far the greater number
of parents and their children.

Molly put the letter on the chimneypiece and went to the dairy—but it was to think about the letter. Her mind kept hovering about it where it stood on the mantle, leaning against the vase with the bunch of silvery honesty in it.

What if Walter was ill! Her father would not be home till much later, and by then there would be no more trains into the city before the slow train in the morning! He might be very ill!—and longing for someone to come to him—his father of course—longing all day long!

Her father was as reasonable as he was loving; she was sure he would never be angry without reason! He was a man with whom one who loved him, and was not presuming, might take any honest liberty. He could hardly be a good man with whom one must never take a liberty! A good man was not the man to stand on his own dignity! To treat him as if he were was to treat him as those who cannot trust in God to behave justly to him. They call him the supreme Ruler! the Almighty! the Disposer of events! the Judge of the whole earth!—and yet they would not "presume" to say, "Father, help thy little child!"

No, she would not wrong her father by not trusting him! She would open the letter! She would not read one word more than was needful to know whether it came to say that Walter was ill. Why should Mr. Sullivan have put his name outside except to make sure of its being attended to immediately?

She went back to the room where the letter lay. Her aunt was still there. She went straight to the mantle, reached up, and took the letter.

"Leave that alone!" cried Miss Hancock. "I know what you are after! You want to give it to my brother and be the first to know what is in it! Put it back this instant!"

Molly stood with the letter in her hand.

"You are mistaken, Auntie," she said. "I am going to open it."

"You shall do nothing of the sort—not if I have anything to say about it!" returned Aunt Ann, and flew to take the letter from her.

But Molly was prepared for the attack and was on the other side of the door before Miss Hancock could pounce.

She sped to her room, locked the door, and read the letter, then went instantly to get her bonnet and coat. There was still time to catch the last train into London! She enclosed the letter in another, larger envelope, addressed it to her father, and wrote inside the envelope that she had opened it against the wish of her aunt, and that she had gone to see if she could help Walter. Then taking some money from her drawer, she returned to Aunt Ann.

"It is about Walter. He is very sick," she said. "I have enclosed the letter, and told him I was the one who opened it."

"Why such a fuss?" cried Aunt Ann. "You can tell him of your impertinence just as well as write it! Oh, but I see you've got your bonnet on!—going to run away in a fright at what you've done! Well, perhaps you'd better!"

"I am going to see if I can help Walter."

"Where?"

"To London."

"You!"

"Yes. Who else?"

"You shall *not*! I shall go myself!"

"And do what, Auntie?"

"Why, nurse Walter, of course—that is, if he *really* is ill?"

Molly knew too well how Walter felt toward his aunt to consent to this. She would doubtless behave kindly if she found him genuinely sick, but she would hardly be a comfort to him.

"I shall be ready in one moment," continued Miss Hancock. "There is plenty of time, and you can drive me to the station if you like. Richard shall not say I left the care of his son to a chit of a girl!"

Molly said nothing, but rushed to the stable the moment Aunt Ann was out of her sight. She harnessed the horse and put him to the little cart, hurrying as fast as she could, in terror lest her aunt should be ready before her.

She was on her way driving the horse from the yard when her aunt appeared, in her Sunday best.

"That's right!" Miss Hancock said, expecting Molly to pull up and take her into the cart.

But Molly touched up the horse with reins, and he, having had no exercise for some time, was fresh and started up at a good speed. Aunt Ann was left standing where she was, thinking at first that the horse had run away on its own; it was some time before she understood otherwise.

Before Molly reached the station, she left the horse and cart at a neighboring inn, then told one of the porters who knew her father well that he was coming by the last train, to look out for him, and let him know that the horse was across the street at the inn. She then boarded and was on her way.

Two hours later, as the train was approaching London, it stopped at a station where another train already stood, bound in the opposite direction, which began to move while hers yet stood still. Molly was looking out of her window as it went past her with the slow beginnings of speed, watching the faces that drifted by in a kind of phantasmagoric show, never more to be repeated, when, in the farthest corner of a third-class carriage near the end of the train, she caught sight of a huddled figure that reminded her of Walter. A pale face was staring as if it saw nothing, but was dreaming of something it could not see.

She jumped up and put her head out of her window, but now her own train was starting to move also; and if it were Walter, there was no possibility of overtaking him, though she was by no means sure that it had been he at all.

The only thing for her to do was continue on to her journey's end!

25 / Home Again

Walter had passed a very troubled night.

He was worse, though he thought himself better. Sullivan looked in to see him before going to the office, and told him that he would come again in the evening. He did not tell him that he had written to his friend's father.

Walter slept through the morning and woke, and slept again. All the afternoon he was restless, as one who dreams without sleeping. The things coming into his mind seemed real, but there was nothing real about them. Late in the afternoon, the fever abated a little, and he felt as one who wakes out of a dream.

For a few minutes he lay staring into the room, then rose and with difficulty dressed himself, one moment shivering, the next burning. He knew perfectly well what he was doing: his mind was possessed with an unappeasable longing and absolute determination to go home. The longing had been there all the night and all the day, except when it was quieted by the shadowy assuagement of his visions. And now with the first return of his consciousness to present conditions came the resolve to act upon what he had been feeling. "Better to die at home," he said to himself, "than recover in such a horrible place!"

On he went with his preparations, mechanical but methodical, till at last he put on his great overcoat, searched his pocketbook, found enough to pay a cab to the railway station, went softly down the stair, and soon found himself in the street—a man lonely and feeble, but with a great joy of escape. Happily a cab was just passing, and he was carried in safety, half asleep again after the exertion of his preparations, to the train station. There he sought the stationmaster, and telling him his condition, prevailed upon him to take a small ring he still had in his possession as a pledge that he would send him the price of his ticket.

It was a wet night, but not very cold, and he did not suffer at first. He was in fact more comfortable than he had been in bed. He seemed to himself perfectly sane when he started, but of the latter half of his journey he remembered nothing but disconnected fragments. What bits of it returned now and then to his recollection appeared as the remnants of a feverish dream.

The train arrived in the town near his home very late in the dark night, at an hour when a cab or other means of conveyance was rarely to be had. Walter remembered nothing of setting out to walk to the farmhouse, and nothing clearly as to how he fared as he trudged along the black country road. His dreaming memory gave him but a sense of climbing, climbing, with a cold wind fighting against him, buffeting him back, and bits of paper, which must have been snowflakes, beating in his face. He thought they were the shreds of the unsold copies of his book, torn to pieces by the angry publisher and sent swirling about his face in clouds to annoy him.

After that came a great blank.

———

The same train had picked up Mr. Colman at a junction on his way home from another direction. The moment he got out, the porter to whom Molly had spoken earlier in the day came up to him and delivered the message Molly had left for him. Surprised and uneasy, he was putting some anxious questions to the man when his son passed behind his back. The night was dark and cloudy with snow, the wind was coming in gusts, now and then fiercely, and the lamps about the station were wildly struggling against being blown out: neither saw the other.

Walter staggered away in one direction, while Richard set out across the street for the inn to retrieve the horse and cart, and then drive home as fast as possible. Only there could he get more light on Molly's sudden departure for London! For in her haste she had not left message enough. But he knew his son must be ill; nothing else could have caused Molly to take such an action! He met with some delay at the inn, but at length secured the horse and was driving home as fast as he dared through the thick darkness of the rough ascent up the hill toward the farm.

He had not driven far before one of those little accidents occurred to his harness which, small in themselves, have so often serious results. The straps of the hames gave way, and the traces dropped by the horse's sides. Mr. Colman never went unprovided for accidents, but in the dark night, in the middle of the road, with a horse fresh and eager to get home, it takes time to rectify anything—with the consequence that he hurried the rest of the way all the more, and paid no heed to the roadside where, invisible to him, another solitary being struggled against the elements.

At length he arrived in safety, quickly undid the horse in the barn and threw a handful of oats in front of him, and hastened into the house. There he speedily learned the truth of his conjecture, and it was a great comfort to him that Molly had acted so promptly.

He himself must be off to London with the first light of morning!

But then, thinking to himself, he realized that by driving to another station some miles farther off, at which a luggage train stopped in the middle of the night, he could reach the city a few hours earlier.

He went again to the stable, quickly rubbed down the horse, provided him with ample feed and fresh water, with plans to leave again in an hour. Then he went back inside and tried to eat the supper his sister-in-law had prepared for him, but with small success. Every few minutes he rose, opened the door, and looked out. It was a very dark night, full of wind and snow.

By and by he could bear it no longer. Though he knew there was much time to spare, he got up to go to the stable to make preparations to be off.

The wind met him with an angry blast as he opened the door, and sharp pellets of keen snow stung him in the face. He had taken a lantern in his hand, but, going with his head bent against the wind, he all but stumbled over a stone seat, where they would often sit on a summer evening.

As he recovered himself, the light of his lantern fell upon a figure huddled crouching upon the seat, but in the very act of tumbling forward off it. He caught it with one arm, set down the light, raised its head, and in the wild, worn, death pale and nearly frozen features and wandering eyes knew the face of his son.

He uttered one wailing groan, which seemed to spend his life, gathered him to his bosom, and taking him up like a child, almost ran to the house with him in his arms. As he went he heard at his ear the murmured words:

"Father, I have sinned . . . not worthy . . ."

His heart gave a great heave, but he uttered no second cry.

26 / Father and Sister Love

Had it not been for that glimpse she had at the station where the last train stopped, Molly would have been in misery indeed when, on arriving at Walter's lodging and being told that he was ill in bed, she went up to his room and could find him nowhere.

It was like a bad dream. She almost doubted whether she might not be asleep herself! The landlady had never heard him go out, and until they had searched the whole house, would not believe he was not somewhere in it. Rather unwillingly, she allowed Molly to occupy his room for the night, and Molly, so that she might start back by the first train in the morning, stretched herself out in her clothes on the miserable little horsehair sofa.

But she could not sleep. She was too anxious about Walter's traveling in such a condition. Yet for all that, she could not help laughing more than once or twice to think how Aunt Ann would be crowing over her: rudely deserted, left standing in the yard in her Sunday clothes, it was now to *her* care after all that Walter was given, not Molly's! But Molly could well enough afford to join in her aunt's laugh. Molly had done her duty, and did not need to be told that we have nothing to do with consequences, only with what is right.

So she waited patiently for the morning.

———

Richard's sister-in-law heard his cry in the yard.

She ran, opened the door, and met him with the youth in his arms.

"I'm afraid he's dead!" gasped Richard. "He's cold as a stone!"

159

Aunt Ann darted to the kitchen, made a blazing fire, set the kettle on it and bricks around it, then ran to see if she could help.

Richard had got his boy into his own bed, had taken off his clothes, and was lying with him in his arms under the blankets to warm him. Aunt Ann scurried about like a steam engine, but noiseless. She got the hot bricks, then hot bottles, and more blankets. The father thought the boy would die before the heat got to him. As soon as Walter was a little warm, Mr. Colman left the house again, mounted his horse, and galloped off to fetch the doctor. It was terrible to him to think that he must have passed his boy on the way, and left him to struggle home without help.

Before his father returned, Walter had begun to show a little more life. He moaned and murmured, and seemed going through a succession of painful events. Now he would utter a cry of disgust, now call out for his father. Then he would be fighting the storm again, with a wild despair of ever reaching home.

The doctor came, examined him, said they were doing quite right, but looked solemn over him.

When Molly reached home, she was received at the door by her father who had been watching for her, and learned all he had to tell her.

Aunt Ann spoke to her as if she had but only the minute before left the room, making not a single remark concerning Walter, and yielding her a position of service as narrow as she could contrive to make it. Molly did everything she desired without complaint, fetching and carrying for her as usual. She received no recognition from the half-unconscious Walter.

If it had not been that Aunt Ann, like other nurses, occasionally had to have rest, Molly's ministering soul would have been sorely pinched and hampered. But when her aunt retired, the girl then had her chance to do her part for the patient's peace.

In a few days he had come to himself enough to know who was about him, and seemed to manifest a preference for Molly's attendance. To Aunt Ann this seemed rather a hard pill to swallow—and hard it would have been but that, through all her kindness, Walter could not help foreseeing how she would treat him in the health to which she was doing her best to bring him back. He sorely dreaded the time when, strong enough to be tormented, but not able to lock his door against her, he would be at her mercy. But he held out a hope that his father would interfere. If necessary he would appeal to him, and beg him to depose Aunt Ann, and put sweet Molly in her place!

One morning—Molly had been sitting up the night with the invalid—she found Aunt Ann alone at the breakfast table.

"His father is with him now," said Molly to her. "I think he is a little better. He slept more quietly during the night."

"He'll do well enough!" grunted Aunt Ann. "There's no fear of him! He's not of the sort to die early. This is what comes of letting young people have their own way! My brother will be wiser now, and so, I hope, will Walter! It shall not be my fault if he's not made to understand! Old or young wouldn't listen to me! Now perhaps, while they are still smarting from the rod, it may be of some use to speak up!"

"Please, Auntie," said Molly, with her heart in her throat, but determined, "please do not say anything like that to him. You might make him ill again. You don't realize how he dislikes being talked at."

"Don't worry! I won't talk *at* him! He shall be well talked *to,* and straight enough so that he won't mistake my meaning."

"He won't stand for it anymore, Auntie. He's a man now! And when he was a boy he used to complain that you were always finding fault with him. But he doesn't have to put up with it anymore."

"Highty, tighty! So the gentleman has the choice when to be found fault with and when not! I've never heard of such a thing!"

"I give you fair warning," said Molly, "that I will do what I can to prevent you from criticizing him!"

Aunt Ann was indignant.

"You dare to tell me, in my own—"—she was going to say *house* but corrected herself—"in my own home, where you live on the charity of—"

Molly interrupted her.

"I shall ask my father," she said, "whether he wishes me to have such words from you. If he does, you shall say what you please to me. But as to Walter, I will ask nobody. Until he is able to take care of himself, I shall not let you plague him with your critical tongue! There now, that is enough said!"

The flashing eyes and determined mouth of Molly, who had risen to her feet and now stood looking at her adopted aunt in a flame of honest anger, cowed her. Miss Hancock shut her jaws tight, and looked the very picture of postponement.

That instant the voice of Mr. Colman came into the room, breaking the silence.

"Molly . . . Molly!"

"Yes, Richard!" answered his sister-in-law.

But Molly was out of the door almost before her aunt was out of her chair.

Walter had asked where she was, and wanted to see her. It was the first wish of any sort he had expressed.

From that moment on he began to improve rapidly. The color slowly returned to his cheeks and he began to take a greater interest in the goings-on about him. Not the least of the new interests he began to feel centered about the ever-present ministering face of Molly.

27 / Walter Wakes From a Dream _____

As Walter improved, he and Molly began gradually to resume their old manner together, wherein they had talked about everything either was thinking. It was a communication Molly had sorely missed, notwithstanding that she and her father shared much the same thing since Walter went away.

One day Walter told Molly the strange dream, which, as he looked back, seemed to fill the whole time almost from his leaving his lodging to his recognition of his father by his bedside.

It was a sweet day in the first of spring. He lay with his head toward the window, and the sun streamed into the room, with the tearful radiance of sorrows over-lived and winter gone, when Molly entered. She was at once blinded and overwhelmed in the sunlight, so that she could see nothing, while Walter could almost have counted her eyelashes.

"Stand right there a moment, Molly!" he cried. "I want to look at you while you are so radiant with light!"

"It's not fair!" returned Molly. "The sun is in my eyes! I am blind as a bat!"

"I won't ask you, then, if it is unpleasant, Molly," returned Walter. In these days he had grown very gentle. He seemed to dread the least appearance of making demands upon anyone.

"I will stand where you like, and as long as you like, Walter! Anything to help you recover your strength."

He smiled up at her, a gentle and contented smile.

"Oh, Walter," Molly burst out, "have you finally consented to live a little longer with us?"

"Of course," he returned. "You don't think I would leave

again so soon after returning home!"

"You don't know what it was like when the doctor looked grave after examining you! We feared that's where you might be bound!"

He laughed lightly. "Not yet, my sister," he said. "I'm not ready for that yet!"

Molly stood where she was for another moment or two, and Walter gazed up at her till his eyes were wearied with the brightness she reflected and his heart made strong by the better brightness she radiated. For Molly was the very type of a creature born of the sun and ripened by his light and heat—a glowing fruit of the tree of life amid its healing foliage, all splendor and color and overflowing strength.

Self-will is weakness. The will to do right is strength. Molly had made a lifelong habit of willing the right thing and holding to it. Hence it was that she was so gentle. She walked lightly over the carpet, because she could run up a hill like a hare. When she caught selfishness in her, she was down upon it to crush it with the knee and grasp of a giant. Strong indeed is the man or woman whose eternal life subjects the individual "liking" to the perfect *will*. Such man, such woman, is a free man or a free woman!

At the moment she had entered Walter's room, Molly happened to be wearing a daring dress of orange and red. Scarcely a girl in London would have ventured to be seen in it, yet Molly looked exactly right in it. Like a dark-cored sunflower, therefore, she caught and kept the sun.

Having beheld her in silence, at length Walter said, "Come and sit by me, Molly. I want to tell you the dream I have been having."

She came at once, glad to get out of the sun. She sat down where he could still see her, and waited.

"I think I remember reaching the railway station, Molly," he began, "but I remember nothing after that, until I thought I was in a coal pit, with a great roaring everywhere about me. I was shut up forever by an explosion, and the tumbling subterranean waters were coming nearer and nearer. They never came, but they were always coming!

"Suddenly someone took me by the arm and pulled me out of the pit. Then I was on the hill above the pit, and had to get to the top of it. But it was in the teeth of a snowstorm! My breath was very short, and I could hardly drag one foot up after the other. All at once there was an angel with wings by my side, and I knew it was Molly. I never wondered that she had wings. I only said to myself, 'How clever she must be to stow them away when she doesn't want them!'

"Up and up we toiled, and the way was very long. But when I got too tired, you stood before me, and I leaned against you, and you folded your wings about my head, and so I got breath to go on again. And I tried to say, 'How can you be so kind to me! I was never good to you?' "

"You dreamed quite wrong there, Walter!" interrupted Molly. "You were always good to me—except perhaps when I asked you too many questions!"

"Your questions were too wise for me, Molly! If I had been able to answer them, this trouble would never have come upon me. But I do wish I could tell you how delightful the dream was, despite all the wind and snow! I remember exactly how I felt, standing shadowed by your wings and leaning against you!"

Molly's face flushed, and a hazy look came into her eyes, but she did not turn them away.

He stopped, and lay brooding on his dream.

"But all at once," he resumed, "it went away in a chaos of coal pits and snowstorms, and eyes not like yours, Molly! I was tossed about for ages in heat and cold, in thirst and loathing, with now one, now another horrid drink held to my lips, thirst telling me to drink, and disgust making me dash it on the ground—only to be back at my lips the next moment.

"Once I was a king sitting upon a great tarnished throne, dusty and worm-eaten, in a lofty room of state, the doors standing wide open, and the spiders weaving webs across them, for nobody ever came in, and no sound shook the moat-filled air. And on that throne I had to sit through all eternity, because I had said I was a poet when I was really not! I was a fellow that had stolen the poet book of the universe, torn leaves from it, and pieced the words together so that only one could make sense of them—and she would not do it!

"Then this suddenly vanished—and I was lying under a heap of the dead on a battlefield. All above me were those who had died doing their duty, and I lay at the bottom of the heap and could not die, because I had fought, not for the right, but for the selfish glory of being a soldier. I was full of shame, for I was not worthy to die! I was not permitted to give my life for the great cause for which the rest were dead. But one of the dead woke, and turned, and clasped me. And then I woke, and it was your arms about me! And my head was leaning where it leaned when your wings were about me!"

By this time Molly was quietly weeping.

"I wish I had wings, Walter, to flap from morning to night for you!" she said, laughing through her tears.

"You are always flapping them, Molly. Only nobody can see them except in a dream. There are many true things that cannot be seen with the naked eye. The eye must be clothed and in its right mind first!"

"Your poetry is beginning to come, Walter," said Molly. "I don't think it ever did before."

Walter gazed at her. How grown she was! What a peace and strength shone from her countenance! Was little Molly going to turn out a goddess in the end! She was a woman, girl, and child, all in one! What a fire of life there was in this lady with the brown hands—so different from the white, wax-doll ends to Lufa's arms! She was of the cold and ice, of the white death and lies. Here was the warm, live, woman-truth!

He would never more love woman as he had! Could that be a good thing which a creature like Lufa roused in him? Could that be true which had made him lie? If his love had been of the truth, would it not have known that she was not a live thing? True love would have known when it took in its arms a dead thing, a body without a soul, a material ghost!

Another time, several days later, they were together again. It was a cold evening. The wind howled about the house, but the fire was burning bright, and Molly, having been reading to him, had stopped for a moment.

"I could not have imagined I would ever feel so at home as I do now," Walter said. "I wonder why it is!"

"I think I could tell you," replied Molly.

"Tell me then."

"It is because you are beginning to know your father."

"Beginning to know my father!"

"Yes. You never came right in sight of him till now. He has always been the same, but you did not—could not see him."

"Why couldn't I see him, wise woman?" asked Walter.

"Because you were never altogether your father's son till now," answered Molly. "Oh, Walter, if you had heard Aunt Ann tell what a cry he gave when he found his boy on the cold stone bench, in the gusty dark of a winter's night! Half your father's heart is with your mother, and the other half with you! I did not know how a man could love till I saw his face as he stood over you once when he thought no one else was near!"

"Is that where he found me, on the stone bench?"

"Yes, indeed! Oh, Walter, I have known God better, and loved him more, since I have *seen* how your father loves you!"

Walter fell to thinking. He had indeed, since he came to himself, loved his father as he had never loved him before. But he had not thought how much he had taken him for granted, both in the past and even now as he lay in his house once more. Thus began a gentle repentance, which had a curing and healing effect on his spirit. Nor did the repentance leave him at his earthly father's door, but led him on to his Father in heaven.

"I know another thing that makes me feel at home," he said to Molly the next day: "Aunt Ann never scolds at me now. Of course, she seldom even comes near me, and I cannot say I mind. But something has happened to convert her tongue. Do you think she's changed?"

"Not that I can imagine. The angels will have a hard time of it before they bring her to her knees—her real knees, I mean, not her church knees! For Aunt Ann to say she was wrong would imply a change I am incapable of imagining. Yet it must come in the end, you know; otherwise, how is she to enter the kingdom of heaven?''

"What makes her so considerate, then?''

"I doubt it's consideration. It's only that I've managed to make her afraid of me, and I told her to watch her tongue.''

28 / Walter Gets a Surprise_____

The days passed. Week after week went down the hill—or, is it not rather up the hill?—and out of sight. The moon kept on changelessly changing, and at length Walter was out of bed and well, though still rather thin and somewhat pale.

Molly saw that he was beginning to brood. She saw also, as clearly as if he had opened his mind to her and spoken plainly, what was troubling him. It needed no prophecy to tell that—he must work!

Yet, she thought to herself, what was his work to be?

Whatever he does, if he be not called to it, a man but takes it up "at his own hand, as the devil did sinning." So whatever work Walter did, it had to be the *right* work!

Molly was one of the wise women of this world—and thus, thoughts grew for her first out of things, and not things out of thoughts. *God's things come out of his thoughts; our realities are God's thoughts made manifest in things, and out of them our thoughts must come. Then the things that come out of our thoughts will be real. Neither our own fancies nor the judgments of the world must be the ground of our theories or behavior.*

This, at least, was Molly's working theory of life. She saw plainly that her business—every day, every hour, every moment—was to order her way as he who had sent her into being would have her order her way. Doing God's things—that is, what God gave her to do—God's thoughts would come to her. God's things were better than man's thoughts, man's best thoughts the discovery of the thoughts hidden in God's things. Obeying him, perhaps a day would come in which God would think directly into the mind of his child without the intervention of things!*

For Molly had made the one rational, one practical discovery of being—that life is to be lived, not by helpless assent or aimless drifting, but by active cooperation with the Life that has said "Live." To her everything was part of a whole, which, with its parts, she was learning to know. She was finding out the secrets of *life* by obedience to what she already knew. There is nothing like obedience—that is, duty done—for developing even the common intellect. Those who obey are soon wiser than all their lessons, while from those who do not obey, even what knowledge they started with will be taken away.

Molly was not prepared to attempt convincing Walter—who was so much more learned and clever than she—that the things that rose in men's minds, even in their best moods, were not necessarily a valuable commodity, but that their character depended on the soil from which they sprang. She believed, however, that she had it in her power to make him doubt his judgment with regard to the work of other people. And that might lead him to doubt his judgment of himself and the thoughts he had always made so much of. Such would be the beginning of wisdom indeed, which had long been her prayer for Walter!

One lovely evening in July, they were sitting together in the twilight, after a burial of the sun that had left great heaps of golden

---

*It may interest some of my readers to be told that I had gotten thus far in preparation for this volume when I took a book from the floor, shaken with hundreds besides from my shelves by an earthquake the same morning, and opening it—it was a life of Lavater which I had not known I possessed—found these words, written by him on a card, for a friend to read after his death: "Act according to thy faith in Christ, and thy faith will soon become sight."

Ed. Note—As readers of MacDonald will no doubt already know, he took pleasure in occasionally stopping his narrative to speak directly to his audience. This is an extremely rare occasion where he speaks, not merely as the storyteller, but as George MacDonald himself, discussing the actual writing of the book! Equally fascinating is this pinpointing of the actual moment when he wrote these words in the month of February of 1887 when a massive earthquake struck northern Italy where the MacDonalds lived. In spite of widespread devastation, including major damage to their own solidly built home, MacDonald was apparently later that very day still thinking of this book, though its progress had so rudely been interrupted. MacDonald's description of the earthquake can be found on page 322 of *George MacDonald, Scotland's Beloved Storyteller*.

rubbish on the sides of his grave, in which little cherubs were busy dyeing their wings.

"Walter," said Molly, "do you remember the little story—quite a little story, and not very clever—that I read to you when you were ill several weeks ago, called 'Bootless Betty'?"

"Indeed I do. I thought it one of the prettiest stories I had ever read, or heard read."

"Why pretty?" said Molly.

"It was so well done! Though I should not say it was perfectly executed, its fearless directness, without the least overboldness, enchanted me. Humble yet forceful, that's how I would characterize its author. Or authoress, I should say! I did, however, detect some mistakes in it. Nevertheless, how one—clearly a woman—whose grammar was not to be depended upon should yet get so swiftly and unerringly at what she wanted to say has remained ever since a wonder to me. But I think I have seen something like it before, probably by the same writer, though I must say it did ring with the tone of a first book."

"You may have seen the same review of it I saw. It was in your own paper."

"You don't mean to tell me that you read the *Field Battery*?"

"We did. Your father went for it himself, every week regularly. But we could not *always* be sure which things you had written!"

Walter gave a sigh of mingled distaste and embarrassment, but said nothing. The idea of that paper representing his mind to his father and Molly was painful to him.

"I have it here—the review of that story. May I read it to you?"

"Well—I don't know—if you like! I can't say I care much for reviews these days."

"Of course not. Nobody should. They are only thoughts about thoughts and things.—But I want you to hear this one," said Molly, drawing the journal folded from her pocket.

The review was very short—long enough, however, to express much humorous contempt for the kind of thing of which it said

"Bootless Betty" was a specimen. It showed no suspicion of the presence in it of the things Walter had just said he saw there. But as Molly read, he stopped her.

"There is nothing like that in the story!" he exclaimed. "That particular statement is completely false, and indeed the whole review completely misses the point of the tale!"

"Not a doubt of it," responded Molly, and went on.

Gradually her reading took on more and more familiarity to Walter's ear, until at length, arrested by a certain phrase he could not mistake, he stopped her again.

"Molly," he said, seizing her hand, "is it any wonder I cannot bear the thought of touching that kind of work again? Have pity on me. It was I—I myself!—who wrote that absurd review! I had forgotten all about it! I am embarrassed to have you find me out in all my poverty of thought! Having you read that review, after all my foolish notions of being a literary man—it makes me feel as the emperor who wore no clothes! I have been very unjust to the author of that piece!"

"You could learn her name, and how to find her, from the publisher of the little book," suggested Molly.

"Yes, a wonderful idea! I will find her and make a humble apology. The evil, alas! is done! But I could—and will!—write another review of the book, this time quite different from the first!"

Molly burst into the merriest laugh.

"You need write no new review, Walter! What you have said is enough."

"I don't understand."

"The apology is made, Walter, and the writer forgives you heartily!"

Walter stared blankly at her.

"Oh, what fun!" exclaimed Molly. "The story is mine!"

Walter's blank expression turned to one of disbelief, as his jaw fell half an inch.

"You needn't stare so—as if you thought I couldn't do it! Think of the bad grammar! It was not a strong point at Miss

Talebury's school! Yes, Walter," she continued, talking like a child to her doll, "it was little Molly's first! and her big brother cut it all up into teeny weeny pieces for her! Poor Molly! But then it was a great honor to have a book published, you know—greater than she ever could have hoped for! An honor only increased by having it reviewed by Walter Colman of the *Field Battery*!"

Walter stared bewildered, hardly trusting his ears. Molly an authoress! In a small way, it *might* be. But did God ever, with anything, begin it thus big without a beginning? Here he was, home again defeated!—only to find the little bird he had left in the nest more successful in his own field than he!

The lords of creation have a curious way of patronizing the things they profess to worship. Man was made a little lower than the angels; he calls woman an angel, and then looks down upon her! Certainly, however, he had done his best to make her worthy of his condescension by his ill treatment. But Walter had begun to learn humility, and no longer sought the chief place at the feast.

"Molly," he said, in a low, wondering voice.

"Yes?"

"Forgive me, Molly. I am altogether unworthy."

"I forgive you with all my heart, and love you for thinking it worthwhile to ask me."

"I am full of admiration for your story!"

"Why? It was not difficult."

Walter took her little hand and kissed it as if she had been a princess. Molly blushed, but did not take her hand from him. Walter might do what he liked with her ugly little hand! It was only to herself she called it ugly, however, not to Walter!

Anyhow, she was wrong—her hand was a very pretty one. It was indeed a little rough with work, but it was gloved with honor! It would be good for many a heart to have hands that were so spoiled! Human feet get a little broadening with walking; human hands get a little roughened with labor. But what does it matter! There are others—after like pattern but better finished—being invisibly made, and to be ready by the time these are worn out, for all who have not shirked the work put before them.

Walter rose and went up the stair to his own room, a chamber carved partially out of the roof, his mind crowded with memories. There he sat down to think, and his thinking led to something else.

Molly sat still and cried, for though it made her very glad to see him take it so humbly, it made her sad to give him pain. But not once did she wish she had not told him.

29 / Better Than Pennies

Later that same day, as he did not appear, Molly went up to find Walter. She was anxious he should know how heartily she valued his real opinion.

"I have got a little poem here," she said, "—if you can call it a poem—a few lines I wrote last Christmas. Would you mind looking at it and telling me if it is anything?"

"So, my bird of paradise, you sing too?" said Walter.

"Very little. I sent it to a friend, who took it, without asking me, to one of the magazines for children. But they wouldn't have it. Tell me if it is worth printing. Not that I want it printed—not a bit!"

"I am beginning to think, Molly, that anything you write must be worth printing! But I wonder that you should ask one who has proved himself so incompetent to give a true opinion that even what he has given he is unable to defend!"

"I shall always trust your opinion, Walter—only it must be an opinion. You gave a judgment then without having formed an opinion. But may I read it?"

"Yes, please, Molly. I never used to like having poetry read to me, but *you* can read poetry!"

"This is easy to read," said Molly, and then began.

> See the countless angels hover!
> See the mother bending over!
>
> See the shepherds, kings, and cow!
> What is baby thinking now?
>
> Oh, to think what baby thinks
> Would be worth all holy inks!

But he smiles such lovingness
That I will not fear to guess!

"Father called; you would not come!
Here I am to take you home!

"For the father feels the dearth
Of his children round his hearth—

"Wants them round and on his knee—
That's his throne for you and me!"

Something lovely like to this
Surely lights that look of bliss!

Or if something else be there,
Then 'tis something yet more fair;

For within the father's breast
Lies the whole world in its nest.

She ceased.

Walter said nothing. His heart was full. What verses were these beside Lufa's empty fireworks!

"A penny for your thoughts!" said Molly.

Still Walter was silent. Indeed, the thoughts passing through his brain were better than gold!

"You don't care for them!" said Molly sadly, but with the sweetest smile. "It's not that I care so much about the poetry, but I do love what I thought the baby might be thinking. It seems so true! so fit to be true!"

"Oh, it is beautiful, Molly! Of course I like your verses!" said Walter at last. "And whatever can be said of the baby's thoughts, the poetry is lovely anyhow! And one thing I am sure of—the Father will not take me on his knee if I go on as I have been doing!—But you must let me see everything you write, or have written, Molly! Would you mind?"

"Surely not! Your father and I used to read everything we thought might be yours!"

"Oh, I can't bear to think of the whole beastly business! I am ashamed of that part of my life! There was not one stroke of good in the whole affair!"

"It may be," said Molly, "that the sort of thing you were

doing was not real—that is, true work—though I'm sure it was hard enough! But all writing about books and authors is not of that kind. A good book, like a true man, is well worth writing about by anyone who understands it. That is very different from making it one's business to sit in judgment on the works of others."

"That is certainly what I was doing for the *Battery*!" said Walter sadly.

"The mental condition itself of habitual judgment is a false one. Such an attitude toward any book requiring thought, and worthy of thought, makes it impossible for such a reviewer to know what is in the book. If, on the other hand, the book is worth little or nothing, it is not worth writing about, and yet has a perfect claim to fair play."

"There is also the matter of one's state of mind when reading a particular work," added Walter, recalling the most painful incident of his recent past.

"Ah, yes! If we feel differently at different times about a book we know—which I know from my own experience—then how am I to know the right mood for doing justice to a new book?"

"I am afraid the object of the reviewer—at least such was the object of *this* reviewer!—is to write, not to judge righteous judgment!"

"One whose object is only to write a notice of a book, and with whom true judgment is the mere pretext for writing, is only a parasite—living off the ideas of others."

"But wherever did you get such ideas, Molly!" exclaimed Walter. "Everything you say is true, but you have never spoken like this before! You could stand among any of the literary men in any gathering in London!"

Molly laughed. "By becoming a critic yourself, Walter, you have turned us into critics—your father and me! We have talked about these things ever since you began writing for the *Battery*. We got as many of the books you reviewed as we could, and studied them ourselves. Sometimes we could not help doubting whether you had seen the true object of the writer. In one you dwelt scornfully on the unscientific allusions, where the design of the book was perfectly served by those allusions, which were merely intended to illustrate what the author meant. We could not help fearing that your critiques and reviews would ultimately prove to be a quicksand, swallowing your capacity for original work of your own. The whole process was a great education for me, and your father helped me to understand many things."

"I continue to be amazed by the Molly I left behind! And you are so right in your assessment! Where my work has not been useless, it has been bad!"

"I do not believe it has always been useless," returned Molly. "Do you know, for instance, what a difference there was between your notices of the first and second books of one author—a lady with an odd name—I forget it? I have not seen the books, but I have the reviews. According to your evaluation of her second effort, you must have, by your first, helped her to improve!"

Walter gave a groan.

"My sins are indeed finding me out!" he said. Then, after a pause, he resumed. "Molly, I am going to tell you about that affair, and all the ugly facts of it—an absolute dishonesty on my part!"

He then told her the story, from beginning to end, of his relations with Lufa and her books; how he had got the better of his conscience, persuading himself that he thought that which he did not think, and how he declared in print that the second of her books was largely worthy, where at best it was worthy but in a low degree; how he had suffered and been punished; how he had loved her, and how his love came to a miserable and contemptible end.

Molly could tell that it had indeed come to an end from the quiet way in which he spoke of it, and his account of the letter he had written to Lufa confirmed her conclusion.

How delighted she was to be so thoroughly trusted by him that he would tell her all!

"I'm so glad, Walter!" she said.

"Glad of what, Molly?"

"That you know one sort of girl, and are not so likely to take the next upon trust."

"We must take some things on trust; otherwise we should never have anything."

"That is true, Walter. But we needn't without a question empty our pockets to the first beggar that comes along! When you wrote that one long letter home, I wondered whether the girl could be worthy of your love."

"I said nothing of her in my letter!"

"Oh, but you did—though not in words!"

"What made you doubt her worth then?"

"That you cared less for your father. Your letters grew gradually more and more distant in tone."

"I have been a brute, Molly! Did he feel it too terribly much?"

"He always spoke to God about it, not to me. He never finds it easy to talk to his fellowman. But I always know when he is talking to God! May I tell your father what you have just told me, Walter?"

"Of course, Molly. Then, if he chooses, we can have a talk about it—just the two of us."

30 / True Work

A few days later, when they were walking outside, Walter asked: "What do you think I am to do now, Molly—in the way of earning my bread, I mean?"

"That is for no one but yourself to answer, Walter," she replied. "You ought to know that."

"I do. But I am still, you know, leaning a little upon the strength of your wings."

She smiled. "Do you still feel as if you had a call to literature?"

"I can imagine nothing else, though certainly the pleasure has been gone from it since the events I told you about."

"Might you imagine nothing else because you have not tried anything else?"

"I don't know. I am drawn to nothing else."

"It seems to me that a man who would like to make a saddle must first have some pigskin to make it of. Do you have any pigskin, Walter, for what *you* want to make?"

"I see well enough what you mean!"

"A man must have a long time for thought before he can have any material for his literary faculty to work with. You could write a book of history, but could you write one *now*? Even for a biography, you would have to read and study about your subject for months—perhaps years. I don't know about your writing poetry. As to the social questions you have been treating, men generally change their opinions about such things when they know a little more. And who would utter his opinions, knowing he must eventually wish he had not uttered them!"

"No one! Unfortunately, everyone is cocksure of his opinion until he changes it—and then he is as sure of it as before till he changes it again!"

"Opinion is not sight, your father says," answered Molly. A little pause followed.

"Well, Molly," resumed Walter, "how is that precious thing, time for thought, to be come by? Write reviews I will not! Write history, I cannot. Write poems I might, but they wouldn't buy enough copies of it to pay for the paper and printing. Write a novel I might, if I had time. But how to live, not to say how to think, while I was writing it? Perhaps I ought to become a tutor or a schoolmaster."

"Do you feel drawn to that?"

"No."

"And you do feel drawn to write?"

"I wouldn't dare to say my thoughts are so valuable that they demand expression. I may have once said that, but no more! Yet somehow I do want to write nonetheless."

"You have said that some authors have their beginnings by writing what is of no value, but come in the end to write things that are precious and held so by many others."

"It is true."

"Then perhaps you have served your apprenticeship in worthless things, and the inclination to write now comes of precious things within you bubbling their way to the surface, things on their way but which you do not yet see or suspect, not to say know!"

"But many men and women have the impulse to write, who never write anything of much worth."

Molly thought a while.

"What if they yielded to the impulse before their time had come?" she ventured at length. "What if their eagerness to write when they ought to have been doing something else destroyed the call in them? That is perhaps the reason why there are so many dull preachers—that they begin to speak before they have anything to say!"

"Teaching would be favorable to learning."

"It would also tire your brain. You would learn chiefly from thoughts, and I am in favor of things coming first, so that we can learn the thoughts behind them. And besides, if you taught, where would be your time for thinking?"

"You have something in your mind, Molly! What is it?"

"I know you will do what appears to you right, whatever I or anyone else may propose. But don't you think that, for the best writing, a man ought to be financially independent of his writing, so that the need to earn a livelihood does not crush the imagination under the foot of the utilitarian?"

"You would have your poet become a rich man before he begins to write!"

"Just the contrary, Walter! A rich man is the most dependent of all—at least most rich men are. Take his riches, and what could he do for himself? Far from independent, he *depends* on his money!"

"I do not see what that has to do with writing, Molly."

"I would see the poet earn his bread by the sweat of his brow—with his hands feed his body, and with his heart and brain feed the hearts of his brothers and sisters. Your father and I have talked a great deal about this. It is one of the meanest and silliest articles in the social creed of our country that a man is not a gentleman who works with his hands. He who would be a better gentleman than the Carpenter of Nazareth is not worthy of him. He gave up his work with his hands only to do better work for his brothers and sisters, and then he let the men and women, but mostly, I suspect, the women, that loved him support him! Thousands of young men think it more gentlemanly to be clerks than carpenters; but, if I were a man, I would rather *make* anything than add up figures or handle money or copy letters all day long! If I had brothers, I would ten times rather see them masons, or carpenters, or bookbinders, or gardeners, or shoemakers than have them doing what ought to be left for the weaker and more delicate!"

"Which would you like to see me, Molly—a carpenter or a shoemaker?"

"Neither of those, but I think rather a farmer, Walter. Surely you don't want to be a finer gentleman than your father! If you ask me, you couldn't do better than to stay at home and help him, and grow strong. Plough and cart, plant and harvest, and do the work of a laboring man. Nature will be your mate in her own workshop!"

What wisdom had not obedience borne in Molly! If Burns had but kept to his plough and his fields, to the birds and the beasts, to the storms and the sunshine! He was a free man while he lived by his labor among his own people. Ambition makes of gentlemen time-servers and paltry politicians. Of the ploughman-poet Burns it made an exciseman, after which his poetry was never the same!

"What will then become of the think-time you say I should have?"

"While you work with your hands, your mind will fill itself with pure and true thoughts. And knowing your father, he will allow you time to pursue your dreams. In winter, which you say is the season for poetry, there will be plenty of time, and in summer there will be some. Not a stroke of your pen will have to go for a dinner or a pair of shoes! Thoughts born of the heaven and the earth and the fountains of water will spring up in your soul and have time to ripen. If you find you are not wanted for an author, you will thank God you are not an author. What songs and poems you would write then, Walter!"

They had made a circle in their walk and had now reached the front of the house. Walter stood motionless, pondering her words. Once he lifted his head as if to speak, but then did not. Molly remained silent. Finally Walter turned and went inside and again to his room.

What passed there, I need not say. Walter was a true man in that he was ready to become truer. And what better thing could be said of any unfinished man!

31 / The Last But Not the End

It was now the second spring, a year later, and Molly and Walter sat again in the twilit garden. Walter had just come home from his day's work, where he had been ploughing in the field. He had become a broad-shouldered, lean, powerful, handsome fellow, with a rather slow step but soldierly carriage. His hands were brown and mighty, and took a little more washing than before.

"My father does not seem quite himself," he said to Molly.

"He has been a little tired for a day or two," she answered.

"Do you think there is anything wrong?"

"No. It is only his spirits. He has never been the same since your mother died. But he declares himself the happiest man in the county, now that you are at home with us."

"His son too is happy to be home . . . and with you!"

Walter was up early the next morning, and again at his work. A newborn wind blew on his face and sent the blood singing through his veins. If we could hear all finest sounds, we might, perhaps, gather not only the mood but the character of a man by listening to the music or the discord the river of his blood was making, as through countless channels it irrigated lungs and brain. Walter's that morning must have been weaving lovely harmonies! It was a fresh spring wind, the breath of the world reviving from its winter swoon. His father had managed to pay his debts, his hopes were high, his imagination active. His horses were pulling strong. The plough was going free, turning over the furrow smooth and clean. He was one of the powers of nature at work for the harvest of the year. He was in obedient consent with the

185

will that makes the world and all its summers and winters! He was a thinking, choosing, willing part of the living whole, a vital fountain issuing from the heart of the Father of men! Work lay all about him, and he was doing the work! And the woman his heart had gradually grown to love with that most blissful of all earthly loves was at home singing about hers! At night, when the sun had set and his day's work was done, he would go home to her and his father and his books and his writing!

But as he labored, his thought on this day was mostly of his father: he was trying to *make* something to cheer him up. The eyes of the old man never lost their love, but when he forgot to smile, Molly looked grave, and Walter felt that a cloud was passing over the sun. They were a true family: when one member suffered, all the members suffered with it.

So throughout the morning, as his horses pulled, and the earth opened, and the plough folded the furrow back, Walter thought and made and remembered: he had a gift for remembering completions and forgetting the chips and rejected rubbish of the poem-making process. In the evening he carried home with him these verses:

How shall he sing who hath no song,
He laugh who hath no mirth?
Will strongest cannot wake a song!
It is no use to strive or long
To sing with them that have a song,
And mirthless laugh with mirth!
Though sad, he must confront the wrong,
And for the right face any throng,
Waiting, with patience sweet and strong,
Until God's glory fills the earth;
Then shall he sing who had no song,
He laugh who had no mirth!

Yea, if like barren rock thou sit
Upon a land of dearth,
Round which but phantom waters fit,
Of visionary birth—
Yet be thou still, and wait, wait long;

There comes a sea to drown the wrong,
His glory shall o'erwhelm the earth,
And thou, no more a scathed rock,
Shalt start alive with gladsome shock,
Shalt a hand-clapping billow be,
And shout with the eternal sea!

To righteousness and love belong
The dance, the jubilance, the song!
For, lo, the right hath quelled the wrong,
And truth hath stilled the lying tongue!
For, lo, the glad God fills the earth,
And Love sits down by every hearth!
Now must thou sing because of song,
Now laugh because of mirth!

He showed it first to Molly. She read the verses, then rose to run with them downstairs to her father. But Walter caught and held her.

"Remember, Molly," he said, "I wrote it for my father, but it is not my own feeling right now at this moment. For me, God has sent a wave of his glory over the earth. It has come swelling out of the deep sea of his thought, has caught me up, and is making me joyful as the morning. That wave is my love for you, Molly— it is you, my own Molly!"

She turned and kissed him, then ran to his father. The old man read the verses slowly, then turned and gave Molly a kiss.

In his heart he sang this song:

"Blessed art thou among women! for thou hast given me a son of consolation!"

And to Molly he said: "I must thank him for this beautiful gift myself! Come," he added, rising, "let us go to Walter."

BETHANY HOUSE PUBLISHERS
Minneapolis, Minnesota 55438

The Novels of George MacDonald Edited for Today's Reader

Edited Title	Original Title
The Fisherman's Lady	Malcolm
The Marquis' Secret	The Marquis of Lossie
The Baronet's Song	Sir Gibbie
The Shepherd's Castle	Donal Grant
The Tutor's First Love	David Elginbrod
The Musician's Quest	Robert Falconer
The Maiden's Bequest	Alex Forbes
The Curate's Awakening	Thomas Wingfold
The Lady's Confession	Paul Faber
The Baron's Apprenticeship	There and Back
The Highlander's Last Song	What's Mine's Mine
The Gentlewoman's Choice	Weighed and Wanting
The Laird's Inheritance	Warlock O'Glenwarlock
The Minister's Restoration	Salted with Fire
A Daughter's Devotion	Mary Marston
The Peasant Girl's Dream	Heather and Snow
The Landlady's Master	The Elect Lady
The Poet's Homecoming	Home Again

George MacDonald: Scotland's Beloved Storyteller by Michael Phillips
Discovering the Character of God by George MacDonald
Knowing the Heart of God by George MacDonald

Sunrise Books, Publishers
Eureka, California 95501

The Sunrise Centenary Editions of the Original Works of George MacDonald in Leatherbound Collector's Editions

Novels

Alec Forbes of Howglen
Sir Gibbie
Thomas Wingfold, Curate
Malcolm
Salted with Fire
The Elect Lady

Sermons

Unspoken Sermons I
The Hope of the Gospel

Poems

A Hidden Life & Other Poems
The Disciple and Other Poems

The Masterline Series of Studies and Essays About George MacDonald

From a Northern Window: A Personal Remembrance of George MacDonald by his son Ronald MacDonald

The Harmony Within: The Spiritual Vision of George MacDonald by Rolland Hein

George MacDonald's Fiction: A Twentieth-Century View by Richard Reis

God's Fiction: Symbolism and Allegory in the Works of George MacDonald by David Robb